GIRL TEN:

WANTED

(A Maya Gray Mystery—Book 10)

Molly Black

Molly Black

Bestselling author Molly Black is author of the MAYA GRAY FBI suspense thriller series, comprising ten books (and counting); of the RYLIE WOLF FBI suspense thriller series, comprising six books; of the TAYLOR SAGE FBI suspense thriller series, comprising eight books; of the KATIE WINTER FBI suspense thriller series, comprising eleven books (and counting); of the RUBY HUNTER FBI suspense thriller series, comprising five books (and counting); of the CAITLIN DARE FBI suspense thriller series, comprising six books (and counting); of the REESE LINK mystery series, comprising six books (and counting); of the CLAIRE KING FBI suspense thriller series, comprising seven books (and counting); of the PIPER WOODS mystery series, comprising five books (and counting); of the GRACE FORD mystery series, comprising seven books (and counting); and of the CASEY BOLT mystery series, comprising five books (and counting).

An avid reader and lifelong fan of the mystery and thriller genres, Molly loves to hear from you, so please feel free to visit www.mollyblackauthor.com to learn more and stay in touch.

ISBN: 978-1-0943-9630-9

BOOKS BY MOLLY BLACK

CASEY BOLT MYSTERY SERIES

BROKEN (Book #1)
FLAWED (Book #2)
BLEMISHED (Book #3)
DAMAGED (Book #4)
TWISTED (Book #5)

GRACE FORD MYSTERY SERIES

NEARLY MINE (Book #1)
NEARLY SAFE (Book #2)
NEARLY FREE (Book #3)
NEARLY GONE (Book #4)
NEARLY HIS (Book #5)

CLAIRE KING MYSTERY SERIES

ONCE HE SEES (Book #1)
ONCE HE LONGS (Book #2)
ONCE HE TAKES (Book #3)
ONCE HE FEELS (Book #4)
ONCE HE KNOWS (Book #5)

MAYA GRAY MYSTERY SERIES

GIRL ONE: MURDER (Book #1)
GIRL TWO: TAKEN (Book #2)
GIRL THREE: TRAPPED (Book #3)
GIRL FOUR: LURED (Book #4)
GIRL FIVE: BOUND (Book #5)
GIRL SIX: FORSAKEN (Book #6)
GIRL SEVEN: CRAVED (Book #7)
GIRL EIGHT: HUNTED (Book #8)
GIRL NINE: GONE (Book #9)

RYLIE WOLF FBI SUSPENSE THRILLER
FOUND YOU (Book #1)
CAUGHT YOU (Book #2)
SEE YOU (Book #3)
WANT YOU (Book #4)
TAKE YOU (Book #5)
DARE YOU (Book #6)

TAYLOR SAGE FBI SUSPENSE THRILLER
DON'T LOOK (Book #1)
DON'T BREATHE (Book #2)
DON'T RUN (Book #3)
DON'T FLINCH (Book #4)
DON'T REMEMBER (Book #5)
DON'T TELL (Book #6)

KATIE WINTER FBI SUSPENSE THRILLER
SAVE ME (Book #1)
REACH ME (Book #2)
HIDE ME (Book #3)
BELIEVE ME (Book #4)
HELP ME (Book #5)
FORGET ME (Book #6)
HOLD ME (Book #7)
PROTECT ME (Book #8)
REMEMBER ME (Book #9)
CATCH ME (Book #10)
WATCH ME (Book #11)

RUBY HUNTER FBI SUSPENSE THRILLER
IF I RUN (Book #1)
IF I TELL (Book #2)
IF I LIVE (Book #3)
IF I FORGET (Book #4)
IF I RETURN (Book #5)

CAITLIN DARE FBI SUSPENSE THRILLER
COME GET ME (Book #1)
COME FIND ME (Book #2)

COME TAKE ME (Book #3)
COME CATCH ME (Book #4)
COME SAVE ME (Book #5)

REESE LINK MYSTERY
BEYOND REASON (Book #1)
BEYOND REACH (Book #2)
BEYOND REPAIR (Book #3)
BEYOND DOUBT (Book #4)
BEYOND NORMAL (Book #5)

CHAPTER ONE

Lucy hated the full moon now, hated it more than she had ever thought she could. Just the sight of it above her as she walked made her shudder. Even so, she made herself walk home along the trail leading from the spot where she'd parked her car back up to her cabin. She didn't want to be afraid anymore.

She was walking through the woods after driving back from the theater production she was appearing in, making her way back along familiar trails to her cabin.

Lucy was slender, almost fragile looking, her blonde hair hacked into short spikes, her blue eyes looking out warily over the surrounding trees, making sure that there weren't any threats there.

Her therapist said that it was important to challenge the assumption that someone would be out to get her every time she went out, that there would be someone waiting to grab her around every corner. It was important to remind herself that she was free, and that she wasn't trapped in the Moonlight Killer's bunker again as one of his "bunnies", waiting to die.

Just the thought of that word made a fresh wave of revulsion travel through her, one that was hard to push back down. It was enough to carry her imagination back to the bunker, where she had been kept as one of twelve women trapped in a deadly game between the Moonlight Killer and Agent Maya Gray.

Thirteen women. Lucy mustn't forget Carmel, who had tried to escape and been killed by the Moonlight Killer for it, her body dragged back into the bunker for the rest of them to see.

Hanratty. Lucy had to remember to think of him by his real name, not by the pseudonym that still terrified her. Michael Francis Hanratty, she had to remember that. Her therapist said that was important, too, to take away some of the power he'd held over her. To remind herself that he was just a man, one who was now safely locked away, where he couldn't hurt her anymore.

Lucy continued down the twisting track that led back towards her home. It wasn't far from the spot where Lucy always parked, but the walk seemed to be taking forever. Maybe that was because Lucy stopped to stare up at the full moon every so often. Maybe it was because she had to step over a tripwire every so often, or past a motion detector. Lucy wasn't taking any chances.

She had to remember that the best revenge was to move on with her life. He'd taken her and the others all at moments when they'd been about to change something in their lives, whether it was getting clean from drugs, going back to school, or finally reconnecting with a loved one.

For Lucy, it had been after she'd finally ditched a controlling boyfriend. She'd even been thinking about an audition for a local theater company. She'd wanted that creativity in her life, but had never dared to do it. Once she'd come out of the bunker, it hadn't seemed so scary. Nothing had, compared to that experience.

So now, she was in a production with a different theater group, trying to make the most of her life. Her therapist had told her to look for anything positive that could come out of her experiences. Well, one thing it had done for Lucy was make her appreciate how important it was to seize the opportunities in front of her. To actually live her life.

Lucy was determined to not let her past define her future, to not let the fear of the Moonlight Killer or any other monster control her life. Still, it wasn't easy.

She'd been there the night Agent Maya Gray had come to rescue her and the others. Maya had been there to rescue her sister, although Hanratty had taken Megan with him when he escaped the bunker. Lucy had never known the terror of being put up as a prize in one of his games, knowing that Agent Gray had to solve a cold case by one of his deadlines, or she would die.

Lucy pushed those thoughts aside, the way she always did, the way she'd learned to do through many months of practice. She needed to get back to her cabin and maybe focus on tonight's performance. There were still a couple of things Lucy wanted to do differently with the part, a couple of lines that weren't quite perfect.

Lucy kept walking back in the direction of the cabin, and she tried to focus on the warm glow emanating from the building. She liked to leave a light burning as a beacon for her when she came home. As she turned the corner, she heard footsteps behind her. Her heart rate increased automatically, so she tried to focus on her breathing, to take deep breaths in and exhale slowly. She had to remember that she was safe.

Even so, Lucy found her footsteps quickening automatically, because why was there someone else out here, in such a secluded place? The footsteps picked up too. Lucy glanced back, her eyes flicking over her shoulder, scanning for any sign of threat.

There was nothing but the forest. Lucy hurried back to her cabin, feeling stupid. She made her way past the security measures she kept in place outside, past the cameras and the motion detectors, rushed inside, made herself coffee, set it down on the kitchen counter, cupping her hands around it for the warmth.

That was when she saw him, standing there.

A dark mass moved in the shadows across her cabin, in a section not lit by the small LED lights of her kitchen. She couldn't make out his face, but her imagination supplied the details. They filled in the face that she'd never seen in person when she was in the bunker, the one she'd only seen at the trial and on the TV. His face. The Moonlight Killer's face.

Except that it *wasn't* the Moonlight Killer coming towards her. As he stepped out of the shadows, Lucy saw that this was a slightly younger man in his twenties. He was taller, more muscular, with short black hair and piercing blue eyes, hidden behind glasses. But the way he held her, the way he looked at her, it was all too similar to the way Hanratty had looked at her through his mask.

She turned to run, heading for the door, her heart racing. But it was no use. He caught up to her in no time, his hand clamping down on her arm with a strength that shocked her.

Lucy opened her mouth to scream, but his hand clamped over her mouth, stopping that too. Lucy had taken a couple of self-defense courses as another way to try to feel safe after everything that had happened. She tried to struggle, to break free, but he was too strong. She was helpless in his grip. It was like a nightmare come to life.

"Did you think it was over, Lucy? Did you think that you were free?"

Lucy felt something jab into her neck, felt the drugs starting to pulse through her system. She kept trying to fight, but now her body wasn't responding, and she could feel darkness starting to close in on the edges of her vision.

"You aren't free," her new captor said. "There's a lot that still needs to happen, and we're only just getting started."

CHAPTER TWO

It was funny, Agent Maya Gray thought, how quickly a happy ending could turn into a desk job.

She sighed and started to work her way through piles of requisition forms, requests for resources, requests to get warrants, schedules. It felt as though she were buried in paperwork, ready to be crushed under the weight of it all.

She was alone in her office. One of the perks of a promotion out to a field office, except that it didn't feel like a promotion when there was no one else there to bounce ideas off. Not that the rest of the field office exactly bustled with life. Through the glass wall of the office, Maya could see a couple of agents working on files, but it was mostly empty. She'd opted for one of the closest field offices to DC, simply so that she could get back home to Marco.

When he was there.

Marco didn't work at the same field office, hadn't been assigned there the way Maya had been. Their superiors had decided that having the two of them working together while they were in a relationship was a potential problem, a conflict of interests that they couldn't allow, so he still worked out of DC, as a field agent. A part of Maya envied him that, even though his undercover work meant that he often wasn't home. She wanted that excitement back in her life.

In between the endless requisitions, Maya started to look through case files submitted by some of the agents she supervised there at the field office, going through the cases, trying to find any places where there was room for them to learn more. Room for her to make a difference to the cases or point them in a different direction.

Maya sighed as she read through one of them, then stepped out of the door, into the office beyond. She wondered what the few agents there would see as she did so. Did they see the all-action agent she had been? The former military intelligence officer? Maybe they just saw a senior agent, high enough up the food chain to give them orders but not truly to be called their boss. Maya still looked the same as she had. She was still tall and dark-haired, with an athletic frame. But she was wearing rather better suits than she had when she was a field agent, and her hair was tied back in a more severe style than before.

"Lewis, get in here," Maya called out, trying to keep some of the disapproval out of her voice.

One of the few agents there stood up, heading to her office with a look of trepidation. Zach Lewis was a young Black man, shorter than Maya was but broad shouldered and with close cropped dark hair. His expression was that of someone called into the principal's office. That wasn't a look Maya had ever wanted to see from someone coming to talk to her.

Maya sat down at her desk, gesturing for Lewis to take a seat opposite her. She turned the case file he'd sent across her desk around so he could see it.

"Is everything okay?" he asked, in a tone that made it clear he knew it wasn't.

Maya shook her head. "I've been reading through your file on the investigation into those gang-related killings. You say you have a suspect."

"A local hit man named Alain Grascini is looking *good* as a suspect," Lewis said. "We've been after him for years, and this time, we have plenty of evidence pointing his way. His DNA on a cigarette butt we found near the scene, a bullet caliber consistent with the weapon he likes used to kill the victims."

"Except that it's all a little too neat, isn't it?" Maya said, trying to get him to see her problem with it. "This guy is meant to be a professional, but he leaves something obvious and easy to find with his DNA on it?"

Lewis shrugged. "Everyone slips up."

"Maybe," Maya said. "But they don't teleport. There are reports from some of the FBI's CIs that Grascini is currently over on the west coast, which means that he couldn't have been there to do this. He also doesn't work for the Toma family, and from what I can see from the witness statements, all your victims are people who appear to have upset the Tomas. Think about it, Lewis."

"You think that this is someone else, looking to frame him so that we look in the wrong direction?" Lewis said.

Maya shrugged. "It's happened before."

She didn't have to mention the cases she'd worked on, forced by the Moonlight Killer to look at cold cases attributed to him. The cases where people had assumed that he was the killer, only for it to turn out to be others.

And then, after that, the copycat killings. There had been plenty of those in the months since Maya had arrested him, although their numbers had dwindled since Michael Francis Hanratty had been convicted. They'd dwindled to the extent that Maya's task force had been closed down, and she'd wound up here.

"So, what are you saying?" Lewis asked.

"I'm saying take another look. Look for someone connected with the Toma family. Or someone connected to the victims in a different way. Someone who would have known enough about Grascini to get close to him and get hold of his DNA."

Lewis nodded, looking serious now, more determined. "Understood, Agent Gray. I'll get right on it."

Maya leaned forward. "Keep looking, Lewis. I have a gut feeling that there's more to this case than meets the eye. Don't close the case until you're absolutely sure that you have the right person."

"Yes, Agent Gray," Lewis replied, nodding his head. He turned and left her office, heading back to his desk outside like he was happy to get out of there.

Maya didn't care. She sat back in her chair, feeling a sense of satisfaction at the idea of doing what she did best: finding the truth. She was good at looking back through cases, good at finding the things that didn't fit, good at trying to find new angles.

It had allowed her to bring closure to many families over the years. It had allowed her to find out the truth about many crimes attributed to the Moonlight Killer. Now, it seemed that her reward was to spend her time looking over other agents' cases in a field office.

Maya sighed and sent a text message to Marco.

Will you be home this evening?

There was no answer, which suggested that Marco was in the middle of something. Maya tried to imagine what he might be doing: going undercover with some criminal organization, out on a raid maybe, in the middle of a chase with a dangerous criminal. Something exciting, at least.

And all the kinds of things that Maya might have preferred to be doing rather than working on paperwork. She wanted to be out there, chasing criminals. She wanted to be in the field. She wanted to chase down killers again.

And worse, she knew where there were killers out there for her to chase.

Maya held off on making the call for as long as she could, the way an addict might try to hold off on that first drink, before finally punching in a number.

Agent Swift picked up. Sorry, Deputy Director Swift now. Maya mustn't forget the promotion she'd gotten after the successful capture of the Moonlight Killer. She was the agent who had run the task force hunting for the Moonlight Killer back before Maya had realized that the kidnapper she was pitting her wits against *was* the Moonlight Killer. A woman whose rise had been unstoppable now that the killer she'd hunted for years was behind bars.

"This is Swift," she said as she answered, as professional as ever.

"Deputy Director Swift, this is Agent Gray," Maya began.

She heard the sigh on the other end of the line.

"Maya, if this is about those three 'unsolved murders' of yours..."

Maya had tried to have the same conversation with her plenty of times before. With all of her superiors, any who would listen. Not that any had. Still, she had to try again, had to set out her case and hope that this time it would be enough. She wanted to be able to investigate those cases, to find the killers she was sure were still out there.

"Swift, the Moonlight Killer kidnapped twelve women. Twelve."

"Thirteen," Swift corrected her, with a faint sigh that suggested she knew where this was going.

"All right, technically, yes," Maya replied, "but the thirteenth kidnap victim was intended to take him back up to twelve after Carmel died. Twelve was the number that mattered to him. Twelves are *important* to him."

"I'm aware of that, Maya," Swift said, her voice stern, obviously anticipating what Maya was going to say next. She'd heard it before, after all. She was probably tired of hearing it by now.

"He planned to release one woman with each case I solved," Maya said, going through it anyway, hoping that, this time, the logic would be impossible to ignore. "The very fact that he tried to replace Carmel means that he *needed* twelve."

"Because you think he had twelve cold cases he wanted you to look into," Swift said, playing her part in the conversation.

"Not just twelve cold cases. Twelve cases relating to him, or at least, attributed to him." To Maya, that was the crucial point. "That's what all the other cases were. Twelve cases wrongly assumed by local cops, and even by us, to be the work of the Moonlight Killer. Twelve kills, or killing sprees, that people thought they got away with."

"Michael Francis Hanratty was convicted of fifteen murders," Swift pointed out, as if that solved anything. "He didn't stop at twelve."

"Or maybe he did," Maya said. "At least with the ones where he killed according to his pattern. The women I rescued meant that he would have been able to force me to investigate three more cases. If all of them were crimes he was later convicted of, that would bring the total down to twelve. His favorite number."

"That's supposition," Swift said.

"It's based on the evidence we have."

"He could have forced you to look into *any* cases, Maya," Swift said. "His, someone else's, ones that he was never convicted of in the end. Which three are meant to be the ones that he didn't do?"

"I... don't know for sure," Maya admitted. That was the hard part of this now. All of the murders Hanratty had been convicted of fit his MO: women strangled on the full moon, usually while they were on the cusp of change in their lives. "I would need to start looking at all the murders to find the ones that don't fit. But that *should* happen. Someone should look, at least. There are three killers out there who haven't been caught."

"And if you start reinvestigating these solved cases? If you do prove that three of the murders he was convicted of weren't his doing, what then?" Swift demanded. "Do you think that some defense lawyer isn't going to come in and claim that *all* the convictions are unsafe?"

"This is about twelves," Maya insisted. She knew how important twelves were to Hanratty. He'd killed more than twelve people, but only twelve victims in his signature style.

"You think that, but can you really be sure about it?" Swift sighed. "I appreciate your dedication, Maya. I really do. But you have a theory, that's all. We can't just go chasing after ghosts. Unless you have something concrete to go on, there's nothing we can do."

Maya nodded, feeling the weight of defeat settle over her. She wasn't going to win this argument. Again. "Understood, Deputy Director."

"Good. Now, is there anything else I can help you with?"

Maya shook her head, even though Swift couldn't see her. "No, that's all. Thank you for your time."

She hung up the phone and sat back in her chair, feeling the familiar frustration and anger boil up inside her. She knew that they were missing something, but she couldn't figure out what it was. And until she did, there was nothing she could do.

Maya closed her eyes, taking a few deep breaths to calm herself down. She couldn't afford to let her emotions get the best of her. She had work to do, even if it wasn't catching three killers she was certain were still out there.

And Marco would be waiting for her at home. She could go back to him, should go back to him and forget about this for now. Even so, there was a part of her that longed to simply pick one of the cases and start to look deeper at it, hoping to find an answer.

Maya barely stopped herself. No, she had to get back to Marco.

CHAPTER THREE

"Marco, I'm home!" Maya called out as she returned to the suburban house that she shared with Marco. It was already getting a little later than she'd intended because, almost inevitably, people had come to her with more urgent case reports to look through right as she was ready to get going.

"I'm just through in the kitchen," Marco called back to her.

Maya smiled at the sound of his voice. Maya could already smell the food cooking: pasta and meatballs, if she was any judge.

Maya could remember the days when she'd come home to an empty apartment, almost devoid of personal touches, now she was greeted with warmth and the smell of a home-cooked meal. The space was filled with Marco's things, and it felt like a real home. She walked through the living room, hearing the TV playing in the background.

She smiled to herself as she made her way to the kitchen, slipping off her jacket and hanging it up on a hook by the door.

"That smells amazing," she said as she entered the room. "What's the occasion?"

As she rounded the corner into the kitchen, she saw Marco standing at the stove, stirring the sauce. As always, it was a sight that made Maya stop and drink it in.

Marco was tall, taller Maya by a good six inches, with a swimmer's body currently encased in a plaid shirt and jeans, with an apron over the top. Either he'd changed since he got home, or he'd been carefully avoiding the standard dark suit that would have made him stand out as an FBI agent.

Marco grinned at her. "Does there have to be an occasion? I just thought I'd surprise you with a nice dinner tonight."

It was right around that time that Maya saw the bruise under Marco's left eye.

"What happened?" Maya asked.

Marco shrugged. "Just a suspect. We were running an operation to bust a couple of drug dealers, hoping that they'll lead us higher up the chain. One of them tried to make a run for it, and then it escalated from there."

Maya winced at the thought of Marco getting hurt, even though she knew that he was more than capable of handling himself.

"You need to be careful," Maya said.

Marco's smile only widened. "As if you would have been?"

He had a point. Maya had jumped headfirst into more than her share of dangerous situations, both in the army and as an agent.

Now, though, it was hard to keep from feeling a hint of jealousy. Marco still got to be out in the field, while Maya was stuck behind a desk most days, not able to do the kind of hands-on investigating that she was good at.

Maya walked over to him, standing on her toes to kiss him on the cheek. "I'm just glad you're okay," she said. "And dinner looks amazing."

They worked together to set the table.

“How did the bust go?” Maya asked. “Aside from getting punched?”

“Pretty well. If we’re lucky, our suspect will turn on the next level above him.”

Maya listened to Marco talk about the bust, admiring the passion he had for his job. She couldn't help but feel a twinge of envy.

"So, how about you? How was your day?" Marco asked as they sat down to eat.

Maya hesitated, not wanting to bring up the frustrating conversation she'd had with Swift. But she knew that Marco would want to know. He was her partner, after all.

"It was...frustrating," she finally admitted. "I feel as though I could be doing so much more than just being stuck behind a desk all day."

"More?" Marco said. "I barely see you as it is."

"I'm not the one who disappears for days on end," Maya pointed out. It was an old argument now, and what did it say that they'd only been engaged for six months, but they already had old arguments? "You don't even take my calls, half the time."

"Because I'm undercover," Marco shot back. "You know what that means, Maya, probably as well as anyone. I don't keep my personal phone on me when I'm doing that kind of work, because one message that doesn't fit who I'm meant to be and my cover will be blown. It could get me killed."

Maya knew that, but it didn't make it any easier to deal with. It felt as though she and Marco were seeing less and less of one another as the months went by. Between his cases and her workload at the field office, it seemed as if their paths only crossed accidentally and occasionally these days. Even on weekends, there was no guarantee that they would find time for one another.

Maya pushed her food around her plate, no longer feeling hungry. "I just wish we could find a way to balance the job and our personal lives. I feel as though I'm always missing out on something."

"I know," Marco said softly. "But we knew what we were getting into when we signed up for this job. It's not easy, but it's worth it. And we'll find a way to make it work."

Maya nodded, not sure if she believed him. It felt as though they had been having similar conversations for months, and nothing had really changed.

After dinner, they cleaned up the kitchen together in silence. Maya was lost in her thoughts, trying to figure out how to make things better between them. Trying to figure out how to bridge the gap that was growing there.

They headed through to the living room, where Marco sat down on the couch with a beer, holding one out for Maya. She took it.

"How about we just take this evening to relax?" Marco suggested. "Maybe watch some trashy TV, you can tell me all about your day, the parts that didn't involve case files..."

If he hadn't suggested that, maybe Maya would have agreed to it. The fact was, though, that her day had been about a hundred times less exciting than his, and she didn't need the reminder of it.

"My day mostly consisted of catching Agent Lewis' mistakes before he could go after the wrong guy," Maya said.

"Sounds like a big deal," Marco replied.

Maya sighed. That was the problem: it was a big deal. Potentially a very big one. What she did was undeniably important, because it mattered whether the agents she supervised were going in the right directions with their caseloads. It mattered whether they were getting the resources they needed and if they could get the legal backup required to let them do their jobs. Because of what she'd done today, a killer might be tracked down, rather than the man who had been framed.

It mattered, and Maya was definitely being paid more for her efforts than she had been as a simple field agent. More than Marco was now that he'd gone from being Detective Spinelli to Agent Spinelli. The boost to her salary was a part of why they got to live in such a nice neighborhood, in a nice house, with good neighbors.

It was just that none of it was where Maya's head was currently at.

"I should work on my book for a little while," Maya said. "It's not going to write itself, and I want to get it finished."

Marco looked a little disappointed, but he nodded. "I get that. I just thought maybe you could take one night off from the writing."

"There's been some interest from publishers," Maya said. There had, of course there had. The tell-all book about the Moonlight Killer by the agent who had taken him down? Who wouldn't want to read that? If she'd finished it, probably it would already have been snapped up.

It wasn't why Maya had said it, though. After what had happened with Agent Swift today, she *needed* to do this, needed to put this work in.

Maya grabbed her laptop and settled into one of the living room's armchairs. She could have curled up on the couch with Marco, but then she wouldn't have been able to concentrate on anything but him, and she needed to concentrate. For this, she had to be able to focus.

Maya opened up the files that she'd made. Files with everything she remembered, files with everything she'd been able to grab from elsewhere. Files that aimed to get all the information for the cases in one place.

There were files for the manuscript, too, although Maya had to admit that those were a bit sparse. It seemed that every time she settled down to write the true crime book that everyone seemed to want, she got distracted.

Marco was still sitting on the couch, flipping through channels, but she didn't pay him much attention. Maya was lost in her writing, reliving some of the most brutal moments of her career.

But, as much as she tried to focus on the writing, her attention was pulled to the files detailing the Moonlight Killer's purported murders. Fifteen files, culled from many more possibilities, by the prosecutors, and by Maya. Maya had been able to show them that a lot of the murders attributed to the Moonlight Killer were simply implausible as his work, that they didn't fit the clear pattern that came out once you filtered out the noise. She'd shown them the real pattern, and that meant that she'd been able to take out the ones where he'd supposedly targeted men, or used some MO other than strangulation, or supposedly killed someone who wasn't close to changing something in her life.

But they'd still settled on fifteen to prosecute him for. Fifteen sets of murders that fit well enough with his patterns to make it hard to tell if it was him or not. Fifteen clusters of lost lives and grieving families who had probably gained some kind of closure in seeing the man who had done this convicted.

Fifteen cases, but Maya was still convinced that it should only be twelve. She couldn't stop herself from going through the files, writing notes, trying to find discrepancies that would allow her to identify three of those cases as the work of someone else. They had to be there somewhere.

She was so absorbed in her work that she didn't even hear Marco get up and walk out of the room, heading for bed. By the time she looked up again, it was nearly midnight. She stretched, feeling her joints pop, and shut her computer down.

She didn't feel any further along than she had been. There were still three cases in those fifteen that weren't the work of the Moonlight Killer, three killers who were still somewhere out in the world, free to kill again.

And she didn't know which ones.

CHAPTER FOUR

Maya was grateful that it was the weekend, given how late she'd worked on her research. Not that the weekend kept Marco in the house.

"You have to go?" Maya said.

Marco nodded. "The guys we arrested gave us a potential lead that might get us a little further up the chain in their organization."

"I could come with you on this one," Maya suggested. She hadn't been out in the field in months now, thanks to her new job. Maybe what she needed right now was the action of chasing after a few bad guys.

Marco smiled and shook his head, though. "I appreciate the offer, but I think it's best if you stay here. You know how the FBI has been about us working together now that we're a couple."

Maya sighed. "That is such a stupid rule."

Marco raised an eyebrow. "Is it? If it came down to a choice between pulling me out of danger or catching a dangerous criminal, which would you choose?"

"That's my point. You *should* prioritize saving your partner in that situation. If any agent abandoned their partner when they were in danger, no one would want to work with them again, but because we're a couple, that's meant to be the wrong thing, suddenly?"

Marco shrugged. "I don't make the rules. Besides, I'm going back undercover. It would look pretty weird if I suddenly show up with you alongside me."

"What? Your cover identity can't have a girlfriend?" Maya countered.

"It's not that kind of operation, Maya. Plus, I figure you're going to want to keep working on that book of yours. The time you're putting into it, it's going to be a bestseller."

Maya smiled wryly, even though it was hard to ignore the implied note of criticism there in Marco's words, the suggestion that she'd been spending her time on her book rather than on him. Or maybe that was just Maya imagining that. Maybe it was her own sense of guilt speaking at letting their relationship drift for the sake of her research.

"Let's hope so," Maya said, ignoring those thoughts.

She watched Marco leave in the same battered station wagon that he'd driven for as long as she'd known him. He could have upgraded from the beaten up old Explorer a dozen times by now, but he hadn't. It was one of the things Maya still loved about him.

Once Marco had left, Maya went back to her files. She was still convinced that there were three murders in the Moonlight Killer's case that weren't actually his work. It was something that she couldn't shake from her mind, but how was she meant to prove that?

The problem was that the information Maya had wasn't going to change. The information in the files was fixed now, with nothing new coming. Michael Francis Hanratty was in jail, so no one was going to do any additional investigation except Maya.

She had done some, talking to a couple of witnesses in different cases under the guise of working on her book, but it was hard to get people to talk to her when she wasn't working in an official capacity, and she hadn't gotten anything new from it.

That should have disheartened Maya, but instead, it took her back to her early days of working cold cases, going through files that had long since been abandoned in a file store or some dusty corner of the FBI's computer systems.

In those days, it had always been about trying to find new ways into the evidence that was already there, trying to find new angles even before Maya went searching for more. She'd needed to look for the ways into the cases before she started to dig for new evidence, because after so long, people were always reluctant to talk.

This was the same, but Maya wasn't *finding* the ways in that she might have hoped for, no matter how she arranged and rearranged the evidence. None of the killings stood out as obviously different from the others. None of them deviated from the patterns that Maya knew the Moonlight Killer favored.

Was it possible that Deputy Director Swift was correct and that there *were* no extra three cases? Was it possible that kidnapping twelve women had all been a way to distract Maya from the truth?

No, she didn't believe that. Twelves were important to Hanratty. He'd told her the reason for it, watching twelve members of his special forces unit die in a botched operation. Twelve men whose lives had been cut short when they'd still had so much potential. Maya didn't think he'd made that story up. It fit with everything else that had come out about him during the trial, and in Maya's research for the book.

Maya had that research in front of her. She started to look back through everything that she'd learned about Michael Francis Hanratty, better known as Frank, or simply as the Moonlight Killer.

He'd grown up on his family farm, where his strangeness and lack of empathy had been focal points for his parents' abuse of him, trying to turn him into what they saw as a normal, well behaved boy.

It seemed pretty clear now that he'd killed them, although their deaths weren't among the ones he'd been convicted of. The main house of the farm had burned, so there hadn't been much evidence. Hanratty had gone into the foster care system, then on into the army. There weren't many details of what he'd done there, because much of it was classified, but Maya had been able to take some educated guesses, based on her own experiences. After that...

Maya's train of thought was interrupted by a knock on the door. She started at it, remembering too late that her sister Megan was due to visit.

Maya hurried over to the door. Megan was standing there, looking bright and happy in jeans and a teal sweatshirt. Her dark hair fell in a braid down her back, revealing the delicate features that had been a part of why the Moonlight Killer had picked her out as a kidnapping victim. That, and what he wanted to force Maya to do, solving crimes on his behalf.

Maya was glad that Megan looked so happy now. Being trapped in a bunker at the mercy of a serial killer was enough to leave deep scars on anyone, but Megan appeared to be moving on well with her life. She'd even re-enrolled in art school, and her work was getting better every day.

Maya gave her younger sister a warm hug and invited her inside. As they settled onto the couch, Maya couldn't help but think about how lucky they were to still have each other. If she had made one wrong move during her investigation of the Moonlight Killer, they might both be dead right now. But they weren't. They were still here, alive and thriving.

"You're looking good," Maya said.

"While you look like you haven't slept," Megan said.

"I just got a little caught up in working on my book," Maya said, with a nod towards the still open laptop. "How are you though? How have you been the last couple of days?"

That was one good thing that had come out of all of this; they were seeing much more of each other than they ever had before. They weren't on opposite sides of the country, Maya focused on her job, Megan just kind of drifting. They'd realized how precious they were to one another and how easily things could change.

Megan shrugged, a little smile on her lips. "It was okay, I guess. I got some good work done in the studio. The new piece is coming along well. I've already had a good offer on my last one, too."

"That's good," Maya said.

"And you're still working on that book of yours," Megan said. "When are you going to let me read it?"

Maya hesitated, because she wasn't sure what her sister would make of the way her book was currently going. She didn't want to admit that she didn't have much written because she'd been focusing so strongly on the three unsolved cases.

"Soon," she finally said. "I just want to make sure I have it right before I share it with anyone."

Megan nodded, and they fell into a comfortable silence for a few moments. Maya was just about to ask Megan about the other people at her school when her phone rang.

She checked the caller ID and recognized the number as belonging to Imogen Carsten, another of the women Megan had been imprisoned in the bunker with. Maya had tried to stay in touch with all of them, both to make sure that they were okay and because she'd needed to for her book.

"It's Imogen," Maya said. "I'll take this through to the kitchen while I make coffee."

"I'd rather have tea," Megan said. "Say hi to Imogen for me."

Maya wasn't sure how much contact Megan still had with the others from the bunker. On the one hand, it was the kind of intense experience that could bind people together for life simply because they were the only other ones who'd been through it. On the other, some people preferred not to be reminded of that kind of event, and being too close to the others might do exactly that. Maya got the feeling that Megan fell into the latter camp.

Maya went through to the kitchen, starting to make tea for herself and Megan while answering the call. To her surprise, it wasn't Imogen's voice on the other end of the line, but that of another woman.

"Hello, is that Agent Gray?"

"This is Maya Gray," Maya said. "Who is this?"

"This is Helen Carsten, Imogen's mother."

Maya frowned at that. Why was Imogen's mother calling on her daughter's phone?

"Is everything all right?" Maya asked.

There was a pause on the other end of the line that seemed to go on for several seconds too long. Maya heard a sob, choked back.

"No... no, it isn't. Imogen... we found her yesterday. She... she killed herself."

The shock of those words hit Maya like a physical blow, stealing her breath away.

"I'm so sorry," she managed, her mind racing. How could this be happening? Imogen had seemed like she was slowly rebuilding her life after the trauma of the bunker. Maya had spoken with her several times over the last few months, trying to offer support and help in any way she could. She had never once suspected that Imogen was struggling so much.

"Do you know why she did it?" Maya asked softly, feeling the weight of her own guilt bear down on her. If only she had realized that something was wrong, maybe she could have done something to help.

"It was that place," Imogen's mother said. "It was like a part of her never really got out of there. I... I wanted to tell you. I thought you deserved to know. I'll send you details of the funeral, but right now, I can't..."

"I understand," Maya said. "If you need anything, please let me know."

She stood there for several seconds after Helen hung up, barely able to process what had just happened. It felt like a failure. Like she hadn't done enough somehow. She'd saved the women the Moonlight Killer took as hostages, but somehow, even that hadn't proved to be enough.

Maya went back through to the living room, knowing that she had to tell Megan the news. When she did so, however, Maya found Megan sitting at her laptop, looking through Maya's research notes. Megan looked up with a look of betrayal in her eyes.

"What is all this?" Megan demanded, obviously angry.

Maya took a deep breath, steeling herself for the conversation to come. "Megan, we need to talk about something."

"We need to talk about *this*," Megan said, pointing to the laptop. "I thought you were writing a book, but all that's here are case files, like you're still running an investigation."

"It's not like that," Maya said.

"It's *exactly* like that. When you said you were writing a book about it all, I wasn't entirely happy, but I figured that you had as much right as anyone, that you could maybe tell the world more about the investigation than me or one of the others. But this... it's over, Maya, you get that, right?"

Maya shook her head. "He was convicted for fifteen murders, but then, why did he have twelve of you in the bunker? He clearly intended-"

"I don't care what he intended!" Megan shouted, a sudden burst of anger coming out from her. "I care that my sister can't let go of her obsession. That you insist on continuing to look at all of that when I'm finally moving on. I... I can't be here right now, Maya."

Megan stood up, heading for the door.

"Megan, wait!" Maya said. She knew that she had to tell her sister the news she'd just heard. "That call, it was about Imogen. She... she's dead. She killed herself."

Megan looked back for a moment, the anger still etched into her features. "All the more reason to let all of this drop, Maya."

She walked out.

CHAPTER FIVE

It was raining the morning of Imogen's funeral. Maya stood there at the graveside with Marco next to her, both of them dressed neatly in black. He'd been able to make it away from work for this at least.

Megan was there, but so far, she hadn't said a word to Maya. It was obvious that she was still a long way from forgiving her for what she'd seen in the research files. She was standing on the far side of the grave in the crowd of mourners, her own grief palpable. Why wouldn't it be? After all, this was someone she'd been locked up with for weeks, who had probably thought that she was going to die alongside Megan if Maya got anything wrong in one of the Moonlight Killer's games.

Imogen's family was there. Her mother was utterly distraught, grief etched into her every feature. She was holding onto Imogen's father, who had his arm wrapped tightly around her as they both stared at the casket in front of them. It was a simple wooden one, nothing extravagant, but Maya knew that wasn't what mattered. What mattered was Imogen, and the fact that she was gone now, taken too soon.

There were some members of Imogen's extended family there, and more people who were presumably her friends. There were more of those than Maya might have expected; she'd always gotten the feeling that Imogen was a relatively solitary person.

Then there were the other women the Moonlight Killer had taken, the ones who were still alive, at least. Maya couldn't help thinking of Carmel and Haley, two young women she'd never had the chance to meet, because both of them had died as Hanratty's captives. He'd killed Carmel, and Haley had killed herself rather than go on there.

The others were there, though, Tori and Saoirse, Katya and the others.

Except one. No matter how much Maya looked around, she couldn't see any sign of Lucy Barnet.

That was surprising, to say the least. Lucy lived locally, not having to come across the country the way that a couple of the others did for this. She'd been in the bunker with Imogen as long as anyone, since they'd both been among the last group Maya had freed when she'd finally discovered the location where Hanratty was holding them. She'd shown up for plenty of other small get togethers with the others in the year since they'd all been freed, so it didn't seem like she was trying to push all of this out of her mind the way Megan was. Even if she were... well, Megan was there. Everyone was, because it was a last chance to say goodbye to someone they were all now connected to forever, whether they wanted to be or not.

Maya put that from her mind for now, focusing on the funeral. The priest began the service, speaking about Imogen and her family and her life. There were several small remembrances from Imogen's family and friends, telling stories about her life, a life cut short.

Maya found herself at the heart of a small group of the others, the ones who had been in the bunker with Imogen. All of them were silent for a moment, and Maya could feel the eyes on her. It felt as though she had to say something. "Imogen was more than just a victim of a criminal. She was a friend to all of us, and we will never forget her. I was able to find her and bring her home, but I wish I could have done more to help her put that behind her. I know that she will be remembered by all of us, no matter how short her life might have been."

With that, Maya stepped back from the group. There was only silence as the rain kept pouring down.

People started to drift away, although more were standing around, obviously sharing stories about Imogen. Maya saw Megan talking to Imogen's mother and went over, hoping to talk to her sister, but Megan saw her coming, turned and headed off. It was such an obvious attempt to avoid her that it made Maya wince in pain. She didn't want to do anything to hurt her sister, but couldn't Megan see that she needed to find out the truth? That, if there were still three murderers out there, she needed to make sure that they faced justice?

"What is it between you and Megan today?" Marco asked, stepping up to Maya's side.

Maya hesitated, wondering exactly how much she should admit about her research or about the strain that had put on her relationship with Megan.

But in the end, she decided to be honest with Marco. "I've been looking into the possibility that there might be more killers out there," she admitted, keeping her voice low so as not to draw attention to their conversation.

"Your theory that there are still three killers out there?" Marco said.

Maya nodded. "I know it's not what Megan wants to hear, or the FBI, but I can't just sit back and do nothing. Not when there's a chance that the same thing could happen to someone else."

Marco nodded thoughtfully, his brow furrowed with worry. "I get it. I really do. But you have to be careful, Maya. If you go down this path, it could put everything at risk. Your career, your safety, and even your relationships."

Maya felt a pang of fear shoot through her chest. Marco was right. She couldn't let her pursuit of the truth put everything she had worked for in jeopardy. But at the same time, she couldn't shake the feeling that there was more to the story than what they had been led to believe.

"I know," Maya said, her voice laced with hesitation. "But I can't ignore this feeling I have. It's like something is pulling me towards the truth."

Marco placed a hand on her shoulder, his expression softening. "I know you want to do the right thing, but you have to remember the costs of that. Megan obviously doesn't want to be dragged back into it all."

"I should go after her," Maya said.

Marco shook his head. "I'll go. My guess is that she won't even talk to you until I get her to see that you're just trying to do the right thing. I'll talk to her, and then I'll head back to work if you're okay getting back home from here."

Maya nodded. She'd guessed that Marco would need to head off quickly after the funeral. She could always call a taxi to get a ride home.

"You go talk to her," Maya said. She looked around at the others there. "I'm going to stay here for a little while."

She wanted to talk to the others there. There was a connection there between them all that Maya wanted to talk to them about and understand more. She'd spent time with all the women the Moonlight Killer had kidnapped, had talked to them trying to make sure that they were okay. Maya felt a responsibility towards all of them, even after she'd helped them. *Because* she'd helped them, but also because the Moonlight Killer had only taken them all captive in the first place because he wanted to play his sick games with Maya.

Maya went up to Katya first. She was slightly built and blonde-haired. When the Moonlight Killer had taken her, she'd been running away from her family, trying to start her life over. She looked healthier now than she had coming out of the bunker, and the last Maya heard, she'd gotten a job helping victims of abuse.

"You know, what happened to Imogen wasn't your fault," Katya said as Maya approached.

"Maybe," Maya said. "But she wouldn't have been in the bunker if it weren't for me."

"That was something *he* chose to do, not you." Katya didn't need to say Hanratty's name for Maya to understand.

"Maybe," Maya said, although she wasn't convinced. "But if he hadn't decided to make me solve cold cases for him-"

"Then it would have been someone else." Katya placed a comforting hand on Maya's shoulder. "Maya, you did everything you could for Imogen, for all of us."

Maya nodded, but she couldn't shake the guilt that settled heavy in her chest. "I just wish I could have protected her better," she said, her voice faltering.

"I know," Katya said. "But you can't blame yourself for what happened. It's not healthy."

Maya knew Katya was right, but it was hard to let go of the guilt that threatened to consume her.

"What happened to Imogen wasn't just about what happened in the bunker," Katya said. "We talked a lot. She had plenty of problems before she went in there. Maybe she was on the verge of finally getting help when he took her. Maybe that's why he took her."

The point of change, the moment that the Moonlight Killer seemed to be so determined to steal from his victims.

Imogen looked briefly pained. "We all like to think that an experience like that will change us. That the fear and the horror and the danger will make us into different people, but really? We're still us. Versions of ourselves, anyway. We have all the same thoughts and feelings that we had before, just with a few more layers of trauma. With Imogen... there's a part of me that wonders if she was always heading down this road."

Maya wasn't sure that she wanted to believe that, however much it might absolve her of some of the blame. Maybe because it would absolve her. Maya didn't want to feel better then. She felt as if she'd owed Imogen so much more.

To deflect attention from that pain, she asked Katya about the other thing that had been bothering her here at the funeral.

"You haven't seen Lucy, have you? I thought she would be here."

Katya shook her head. "No, I was talking about that with some of the others. I haven't seen her today. Haven't heard from her in a few days. No one else seems to have, either."

"Is that usual?" Maya asked, because it didn't fit with her experience of Lucy.

Again, Katya shook her head. "We talk a lot. And she wouldn't miss this. She just wouldn't. She and Imogen were friends. She would want to be here."

Which made it all the stranger that Lucy wasn't there. Maya was due to go back into work later, but not just yet. In the meantime, maybe she would take the time to make sure that Lucy was okay.

CHAPTER SIX

"If you get this message, call me, Lucy," Maya said, leaving yet another voicemail message on Lucy Barnet's phone.

She was sitting in the living room of her and Marco's suburban home, getting more worried by the moment. Okay, so Lucy liked to live away from people now. Okay, so she might have missed one message, but half a dozen?

Maya couldn't shake the feeling that something was wrong. A former hostage of the Moonlight Killer suddenly not answering any messages after the funeral for another victim was too much of a coincidence.

Even so, she tried to tell herself that maybe it didn't mean anything. If Lucy had been close to Imogen, then maybe the fact that she hadn't been at the funeral wasn't a sign of something being wrong, but simply that she couldn't face going to it. Maybe the fact that she wasn't answering her calls was down to the same thing. Maybe she couldn't bring herself to answer calls from Maya so soon after the news of Imogen's death.

Maybe, but even that was worrying enough that Maya felt as though she should check up on Lucy. She didn't want to risk the possibility that Lucy was so wrapped up in grief over Imogen's death that she was going to do something to hurt herself. Maya wasn't sure if she could stand that happening to two of the young women from the bunker one so soon after another.

Maya put in another call then, to Imogen's mother, Helen. The other woman picked up after a few rings, her voice obviously wracked with grief.

"Agent Gray, can I do something for you?"

"I'm sorry to call you at a time like this," Maya said. "But I need to check something. You called Lucy Barnet to tell her that the funeral was today?"

"You're calling to ask me that? Now?"

"I'm so sorry to do it," Maya said. "But I think it could be important. Did you call her?"

"I called her, but I couldn't get through. It just went straight to voicemail."

"Thank you," Maya said. "That's all I needed to know. Again, I'm so sorry for your loss."

Maya put down the phone. In a way, the news that Imogen's mother hadn't gotten through to Lucy was even more worrying. It meant that she wasn't just hiding at home, so consumed by grief that she couldn't bring herself to face the world. She didn't know that Imogen was dead, presumably, which meant that she had to be out of contact for another reason.

Maya went to Lucy's social media next, just in case there was a reason that she might be out of contact. Maya kept an eye on Lucy the way she did with all the other women who had escaped Hanratty's clutches. Maya wanted to make sure that they were all safe.

There were the same posts that there had been about the play that Lucy was appearing in, but nothing from the last couple of days. That was strange, because before that, Lucy had been posting regularly, trying to drum up more interest in the performance.

Maya tried to tell herself that it might be nothing, but even so, her worries were building to a level where Maya knew that she had to act on them, just to be sure that Lucy was safe.

Maya needed to go check on Lucy in person. That meant driving out to her cabin in the woods.

Maya quickly put on her shoes and grabbed her keys. She knew that she wouldn't be able to rest easy until she saw Lucy safe with her own eyes.

Maya went out to her car and started to drive over, heading out of Washington DC and into the countryside beyond. Lucy lived in a cabin in a small stretch of forest, away from the city. It seemed that after everything that had happened, she didn't feel safe around too many other people.

As Maya drove down the dirt road towards Lucy's cabin, she couldn't help but feel a sense of unease. She had been down this road a few times before, but this time it felt different. The forest seemed darker and more ominous than usual, and the silence was almost deafening. Maya reminded herself that she was overreacting - she was a trained FBI agent, after all, and a former soldier. She had faced much worse than a cabin in the woods.

Of course, she'd also come pretty close to death in Michael Francis Hanratty's cabin, but this wasn't the same. At least, Maya hoped that it wasn't.

Getting to the cabin meant parking by the road a little way away then walking up a woodland track. Maya was a little relieved to see Lucy's car there, familiar from Maya's previous visits. Maybe there was nothing wrong after all. Maybe Maya was worrying for nothing. Maya got out of her car and set off up the path that led to the cabin.

The woods were beautiful, and Maya could understand why someone who had been through a traumatic experience might want to live out there, away from other people. Maybe it was easier to process some of that trauma when there weren't other people nearby, or maybe Lucy simply felt as though other people were too much of a threat after everything she'd been through.

Maya kept making her way along the path, and that was when her trained eyes caught the faint gleam of something strung across the way. It was a tripwire, apparently made from fishing twine. Maya traced it back and was relieved to find that it wasn't attached to anything dangerous. The Moonlight Killer had been fond of using claymore mines and other booby traps. This just appeared to connect to an alarm.

Maya guessed that Lucy had put it there. It spoke to a level of paranoia about her safety rather than being the kind of trap an intruder might leave behind. Maya kept walking, keeping a careful watch for more such early warning systems. She spotted a couple of cameras hidden in the trees, a couple of motion detectors, too. Maya didn't bother to avoid them. If Lucy was home, Maya wanted to give her plenty of warning that she was coming. She would feel safer that way.

As she grew nearer to the cabin, Maya's heart rate picked up. Something about the way the forest was silent was making her uncomfortable. Her military experience had taught her to trust her gut instincts, and her gut was telling her that something was wrong. As she approached the cabin, she noticed that something was off.

The door was slightly ajar. Her hand instinctively reached for her sidearm as she moved closer. She pushed the door open and stepped inside, looking around in the dim light let in by windows that still had the curtains drawn. That was another strange sign.

Maya considered her options. She could search the cabin in silence, in case there was some threat, but she knew that would probably freak Lucy out if she was there. Besides, if there was a threat, and Lucy was there, Maya needed to know about it quicker than that.

"Lucy?" she called out, her voice echoing through the silent cabin. There was no response.

Maya's eyes slowly adjusted to the dim light filtering in through the windows. She swept the room with her gun in hand, checking the corners and the shadows. Everything seemed to be in order, but her instincts were telling her otherwise.

She moved deeper into the cabin, her steps slow and measured. Maya's brain kept trying to provide her with scenarios in which all of this was just her overreacting and in which everything was fine. Maybe Lucy had just gone out into the woods for a walk. Maybe she'd heard about Imogen's death somehow and had decided she couldn't be around people for a while. Maybe she would come through the door even as Maya searched the cabin for her, demanding to know what she was doing there.

Maya didn't believe any of that. There was something wrong here; Maya just didn't know what, yet. She opened a few of the curtains, letting a little more light into the cabin.

The whole place was silent and still, completely empty. A single coffee cup sat on a kitchen counter, still filled with coffee. Maya touched the side of the cup, testing it. It was cold. Did that just mean that Lucy had stepped outside and forgotten about it, or did it mean something worse?

Maya swept the cabin carefully, wanting to make sure that she didn't miss anything. There was no sign of forced entry. Everything appeared to be in place, but there was no sign of Lucy.

Except... not everything was quite in place. There were scuff marks on the floor, where some of the furniture had been moved. There was a small indentation in one of the rugs where a chair would normally be, but that chair was a couple of feet away in a new spot. It was as if all the furniture had been moved around. Or maybe, just maybe, knocked over in a struggle and put back not quite perfectly?

Maya's heart began to race as she realized that something terrible might have happened to the young woman. She knew that Lucy was a survivor simply because of all that she had survived, but she also knew that there were dangerous people out there.

Maya decided to check the security cameras outside of the cabin, hoping that they had recorded something that would shed light on Lucy's disappearance. They seemed to feed through to a central box in the cabin. Maya checked the footage, but there was no sign of anyone on the footage, no sign that anyone had tripped any of the motion sensors either.

Maya left the cabin, starting to sweep the woods for any sign of Lucy.

"Lucy!" she called out. "Are you out here? It's Maya!"

Maya's voice echoed through the silent woods, but there was no response. The trees were thick, casting shadows in every direction. Maya slowed her pace, her hand still on her gun, and listened. Her heart thudded in her chest as she waited for a response.

There was nothing. Maya started to walk a spiral around the cabin, moving in widening circles, using the sun above as a way to keep track of her direction. Maya knew how easily people got turned around in places where they couldn't keep track of their orientation, but her military training helped her here. She circled the cabin, looking not just for Lucy, but for any tracks, any sign of where she might be.

There were some scuffed footprints on the approach to the cabin, nothing distinct, but enough to suggest that someone had been there. Lucy, or someone else, trying to find a route that would avoid the cameras? A little further along, Maya found scrapes in the dirt, as if someone had been dragging something.

Maya didn't know what to make of it all, but it was undeniable that Lucy wasn't there. She'd either left, or been taken from, her cabin in a hurry, leaving her unfinished coffee behind. That didn't feel characteristic. Lucy struck Maya as the kind of person who would wash up that mug even if she was leaving quickly, someone who wanted things looked after precisely.

Then there was the question of Lucy's car still being there. If she'd left, if she'd just gone away, wouldn't she have taken her car? Wouldn't there be some sign of her on the cameras along the path?

It was a mystery, and one that Maya didn't like.

Maya took out her phone, putting in a call to the local police.

"Hi, this is Agent Maya Gray, with the FBI. I'd like to report a missing person."

CHAPTER SEVEN

"Lucy Barnet is missing," Maya said.

She was back home by now. To her surprise, so was Marco, although it didn't look as though he would be for long. He had a bag packed, waiting by the door.

"When you say that she's missing..."

"She wasn't at the funeral, so I went over to her place."

Marco frowned at that. "You went over to her place just because she wasn't there at the funeral? Lucy wasn't Imogen's family, Maya. Maybe she didn't feel like it was right to be there."

Maya didn't believe that. She *hadn't* believed that. "Lucy and the others built up a bond in the bunker. She would have been there if she could have been."

Marco nodded. "The bunker was a traumatic experience for all of them, but not everyone wants to revisit that trauma, Maya. Megan doesn't."

Maya had almost forgotten that Marco had gone after her sister at the funeral, since she hadn't wanted to talk to Maya.

"How is Megan?"

"She's upset," Marco said. "She told me all about your research. I thought you were writing a book about what happened with the Moonlight Killer, but it sounds like you're still trying to chase his cold cases again. Do you really want to do that, Maya?"

"I am writing my book," Maya insisted. "It's just... those three cases don't make any sense."

"And the fact that you're going after them is hurting your sister, Maya," Marco said.

"I know that," Maya said. "Do you think I don't know that? It's just... there are still three killers out there. I'm sure of it. And now, Lucy has gone missing."

Marco didn't look convinced. "Those things don't have to be connected. And we don't even know that Lucy is missing. She could have decided to get away for a few days. She could have decided that she couldn't handle being at the funeral and left."

"I know that, but this is different," Maya said, shaking her head. "I went to her cabin. Lucy's car was outside her cabin and there was no sign of a struggle, but she's gone. Her things are still there, but she's not."

"I know what you're thinking," Marco said. "You're thinking that this is Hanratty again. But he's in prison, Maya. My guess is that if there's no sign of a struggle, there was no struggle. Did she have any security?"

Maya had to nod in answer to that. "Lucy had a lot of security near the cabin. Cameras, motion sensors, even a few tripwires rigged to alarms."

"And had any of that been disturbed?" Marco asked.

"No, but that might just mean that whoever did this was a professional. Hanratty is ex-special forces."

"And in jail," Marco repeated.

Which meant that it couldn't be him directly, but he had people, didn't he?

"We know that he had at least one of his victims taken by other people," Maya pointed out.

Marco shook his head.

"We don't know that for sure. We don't have any evidence of that. The most likely scenario is that Lucy walked past her own security because she didn't want to be in the cabin. Maybe she's out in the woods, trying to get her head straight."

"Maybe," Maya said, still not convinced.

"You're grasping at straws, Maya. This could be anything. Maybe Lucy went on a trip and forgot to tell anyone. Maybe she left voluntarily for personal reasons. We can't jump to conclusions without evidence."

Maya knew that Marco was right. She couldn't let her emotions cloud her judgment. But the thought of Lucy being in danger, being taken like so many of Hanratty's victims, was too much for her to bear. She felt as though she had to do something.

"You reported all of this to the local cops, right?" Marco said.

Maya nodded. "But I'm not sure what they're going to be able to do."

"They can organize a proper search for her, for one thing," Marco pointed out. "Look, I have to go. My case is getting more complicated, and I'm not going to be back for a few days."

"Are you going to be safe?" Maya asked him.

"I hope so," Marco replied. "I need to be when I have you to come back to. In the meantime, maybe work on making your book what you said it was going to be, rather than just a way to keep working on those cold cases. You need to let the authorities handle the search for Lucy."

Maya bit her lip, feeling frustrated. She knew that Marco was right. She was letting her emotions and instincts get the better of her.

"All right." It was going to be hard to live up to that, hard to just let the local cops get on with their jobs, but Maya knew that she had to do it.

"I'll see you soon," Marco said, briefly putting his arms around Maya. "I love you."

"I love you too."

Maya watched as Marco walked out of their home, her thoughts still on Lucy's disappearance. It was still odd that a single cup of coffee had been waiting on the counter, that the front door of the cabin had been ajar.

Was it possible that Marco was right? Was it possible that Lucy had simply walked out without looking back, having heard the news about Imogen? Maya wasn't sure if she believed that. She thought that even someone utterly distraught might take something with them, or walked down to her car and driven off. If she'd been so distraught that she hadn't been thinking straight... well, wouldn't she have tripped some of the security measures?

Then there were the scrapes Maya had found in the dirt to consider, the half-worn away footprint. Had that been Lucy's footprint, or someone else's? If it wasn't hers, how had someone avoided setting off the security systems?

Maya pushed those thoughts to the side, trying to do what Marco had recommended and focusing on her book. Maybe if she could make it the true crime book that she'd said it was going to be, she could show that to Megan, show her that she was moving on from her obsession with the Moonlight Killer and his murders.

Maya sat down at her desk, opening her laptop and beginning to type. She focused on the task at hand, letting her mind drift away from the troubling thoughts of Lucy's disappearance. The click-clack of the keys filled the room as Maya typed out the details of the Moonlight Killer's case, the murders he had committed, and the evidence that had led to his capture.

As she typed, Maya couldn't help but think about how different her life was now than when she had first caught the Moonlight Killer. Back then, she had been a field agent with something to prove. Now, she was a more senior agent, forced to ride a desk and check on other agents' work. This book felt like the memories of someone Maya used to be.

Even so, Maya forced herself to keep working. She read through the few pages she'd managed to write, feeling the lack of inspiration that had plagued her writing for months. She couldn't focus on anything else while she was convinced that three killers were still out there in the world, but Maya needed to do that now if she was going to show Marco and Megan that she wasn't simply looking for a way to indulge her obsession.

So Maya kept writing, working on getting her thoughts and feelings down for each stage of the case, trying to remember the different people she'd talked to in the investigations she'd conducted to solve the cold cases the Moonlight Killer wanted investigating. Maya tried to recall the precise moment, somewhere on the second case, when she'd started to suspect that it was the Moonlight Killer she was being forced to work for.

There was something strangely cathartic about the process of writing it all down, trying to get the horrific events of a year ago into some kind of order, trying to trace all the ups and downs she'd gone through in investigating both the cold cases and the kidnappings that had been used to force her to look at them.

Maya felt her fingers flowing over the keyboard for the first time in what felt like forever. She was starting to get into the rhythm of the work, starting to feel what had to come next, and how she had to tell this story so that it all hung together...

A knock at the front door to the house interrupted Maya's train of thought, sending her hurrying to set the laptop aside and move to the door to see who it was. A look through the door's spy hole made Maya frown in sudden worry. She couldn't see anyone there. Was it just kids playing a game, or was it something else?

Instinct made Maya grab her gun, holding it flat against the door as she opened it, just in case. There had been enough attention on the Moonlight Killer case that she'd had a few threats from cranks, and Maya was sure that some of the people who had helped him over the years were still out there. Most of them probably hadn't known or cared who they'd done work for, but Maya needed to be careful anyway, just in case.

Maya opened the door slowly, keeping her gun at the ready. She peered out into the afternoon light, looking over the suburban neighborhood beyond.

That was when Maya looked down and saw the postcard, her heart feeling as if it stopped in her chest.

"No," Maya breathed. "No, not again. This is *done*."

Slowly, she crouched to pick up the postcard. It had none of the whimsical drawings of bunny rabbits that the Moonlight Killer had favored in his challenges and threats. Instead, it was a picture of some coastal town with the words "Greetings from Ellonsea" across the front. Maya looked around for anyone who might have left the postcard there, but there was no one. A couple of her neighbors were out walking her dog, but Maya doubted very much that they had done this.

She picked up the postcard, taking it back inside with her and making sure that the door was firmly locked. Maya took the postcard back to her laptop, sitting down with it before she turned the postcard over, reading the lines on the back.

In one sense, it was a relief to see that the writing wasn't Hanratty's. Maya knew that writing so well now that it was impossible to mistake this for it. This was looping and cursive, even the choice of words different.

I have Lucy Barnet. You're going to solve a case for me. This case. You have until midnight, three days from now. Succeed, and you get her back. Fail, and she will die. Try to find us, and she will die.

Those words made Maya freeze with worry. She'd known that something had happened to Lucy, but the prospect of what might be about to happen to her was terrifying.

Her first thoughts were for Lucy, but her second ones were all about the words there. The words weren't the ones that the Moonlight Killer would have used. Even so, there were similarities in the lack of detail given about the case, the need to work that out a part of the puzzle the kidnapper wanted her to solve.

What case? Maya turned the card back over, and knew at once. Ellonsea was the town where one of the fifteen murders attributed to the Moonlight Killer had taken place. She already had the details of it all in her files.

Was she dealing with a copycat, then? One she and her taskforce hadn't picked up in the months following Hanratty's arrest? Maybe it was even someone who knew him, one of those people who seemed to have been all too willing to provide a serial killer with assistance for a price.

Maya kept staring at the postcard, wondering if she should call it in, tell Marco, tell Swift, tell anyone who would listen.

Maya wasn't sure, not when the consequences specified on the postcard were so clear.

Yet there was one thing she absolutely needed to do right now, one person she needed to talk to.

CHAPTER EIGHT

Maya shuddered as she waited in the interrogation room for the Moonlight Killer.

The interrogation room sat deep in the correctional facility, attached to a wing intended for the most dangerous prisoners. Michael Francis Hanratty was definitely that. This was a man who had all the skills he needed to kill with whatever came to hand, even if he had always strangled his victims with a rope under the full moon.

Two guards escorted him into the room. He wasn't limping now, in spite of the fact that Maya had shot him while arresting him. He'd obviously recovered well in the year he'd spent there. He was a little taller than Maya, athletically built, his dark hair Graying, his cold blue eyes fixed on Maya as he walked in. The sleeves of his orange prison jumpsuit were rolled up, revealing the tattoo on his forearm of a snake devouring an armadillo under the full moon.

"Hello Maya," he said, as the guards fixed his shackles to the table. He sat opposite her, still not looking away while the guards left.

"We'll be just outside," one of the guards assured Maya.

"I'll be fine," Maya replied, simply because she didn't want to give the Moonlight Killer the satisfaction of seeing her worried.

The guards left.

"Hello, Frank," Maya said. "You still prefer Frank, right?"

"Here to get notes for your book?" Frank asked.

Maya frowned. "How do you know about my book?"

Frank fixed her with a level stare. "I still hear things, Agent Gray. People still talk to me." He paused. "This is where you ask who, and I refuse to tell you, so you start looking at all my visitors and phone calls."

"Or we skip all of that," Maya said. She took out the postcard she'd been left. "Why don't you tell me about this, instead."

She saw Frank's eyes on it. There was the barest flicker of interest there.

"It's not one of mine," he said. "Why don't you tell me about your life now, Maya?"

"Why don't you tell me about the postcard?" Maya countered.

"Your life," Frank said, with no give in his tone. "If you're going to come visit me, I think the least you should do is take the time to talk to me a little."

"We aren't friends, Michael," Maya said, reverting to his first name simply because she knew it would irritate him.

It did. Frank's stare became even colder.

"Michael died a long time ago. I haven't seen him in years. And if you won't tell me about your life, then maybe I should. You've been promoted to a job that bores you. You sit around, wondering if you'll ever do anything as important in the field again as catching me. Your sister-"

"Talk about Megan and I'll leave," Maya said. This was a contest of will, one that Maya knew that she needed to win.

"No, you won't," Frank said, "because you still want me to tell you about that." He nodded towards the postcard.

"*Can* you tell me anything about it?" Maya asked.

Frank nodded. "I can."

"And will you?"

"If you tell me how your sister is. Not otherwise."

Maya thought about making good on her threat by walking out. But she couldn't deny that the postcard was too important to ignore. It was the only lead she had in finding Lucy before it was too late. She took a deep breath, trying to keep her emotions in check. "Fine, my sister is fine."

"The truth, Maya."

"What do you want from me? Megan is traumatized. You kept her in a bunker for months. Earlier today, she had to go to the funeral of a woman who was imprisoned there with her. A woman who killed herself because of everything that happened to her."

"If you're waiting for me to feel guilty, you'll be waiting a long time." Expecting a psychopath like Frank to feel remorse was asking far too much.

"I've played your game, told you what you want to know. Now, tell me about the postcard."

Frank was silent for a few more seconds. "You can see, of course, that this isn't me?"

Maya nodded. "Whoever sent this got the details wrong. They didn't hand draw the postcard. The writing is wrong, and the tone."

Frank nodded slowly, like a teacher acknowledging the efforts of a student.

"This person wants me to investigate a case. The murder in Ellonsea. Do you know who it is?"

Frank smiled at Maya cryptically. "The man who took dear Lucy, or the one who killed... what was her name again?"

"Rose Kallen," Maya supplied. She hadn't even had to look at her files for that. She knew the basics of all fifteen of the Moonlight Killer cases by heart. She had no doubt that Frank did, too, and not just for the crimes he'd committed. He'd known all about the cases he'd sent for her to look into.

"In any case, the answer to both questions is yes," Frank said.

"You know who kidnapped Lucy?" Maya said.

Frank shrugged. "I can hazard a guess."

"Tell me."

Predictably, Frank shook his head. "Now, where would the fun be in that?"

Maya clenched her jaw in frustration. She knew that getting information out of Frank was like pulling teeth, but she had to keep trying if she wanted to find Lucy before it was too late. "What's your guess?" she asked through gritted teeth.

Frank shook his head again. "No, that isn't how this works. The game is the same as mine would have been, and I'm inclined to go along with it. After all, you would be proving my innocence."

"Of one crime," Maya snapped back.

Maya glared at Frank. She was running out of patience, and he knew it.

"Fine," she said, crossing her arms. "Let's talk about this Ellonsea murder then. What can you tell me about it?"

Frank leaned back in his chair as far as his chains would allow, his eyes narrowing.

"Murders," Frank said. "There has been more than one."

"But not by you?" Maya asked.

Frank shook his head. "Ellonsea was not mine. I have not been there. I had planned to make you look into it next, before things came to a head."

That was such a polite euphemism for the battle to the death that had broken out between the two of them when Maya had worked out where his hidden bunker was.

Maya felt a brief wave of excitement as she realized that she knew one of the cases now that could be eliminated from the fifteen ascribed to Frank.

"Which are the other two that aren't yours?" Maya asked.

Frank shook his head again, though.

"Everything in its own time. For now, you need to focus on Ellonsea. Judging by the card, time is already ticking down."

"Can you tell me anything else about the killer there?" Maya asked. "Is it someone deliberately copying you, or something else?"

"Because they strangled a woman under the full moon?" Frank said, in a faintly mocking tone. "So many women get strangled. Occasionally, it happens under the moon. I can tell you that the person who committed it was a master of the art. The crime scene was practically pristine. Not a single fiber or hair left behind. And the victim..."

He trailed off, his eyes glinting with something that looked almost like amusement. Maya leaned forward, intrigued despite herself.

"What about the victim?" she prompted.

Frank's lips twisted into a smirk. "I might have chosen her as my own victim if I'd seen her. So fragile. Right on the cusp of change. But no, I don't have anything to tell you about her."

Maya leaned back in her chair, processing this information. "Do you have any leads that you can actually *give* me on who the killer might be?"

Frank shrugged. "I have my suspicions, but I would rather watch you work, Maya. It will be like old times."

"You don't have a bunker full of surveillance equipment to monitor me with this time," Maya pointed out.

"I'm sure I'll still hear what happens," Frank said, with a faint, gnomic smile that gave nothing away.

"And I haven't said yet that I'm going to take this case."

"Of course you are, Maya," Frank said. "What else will you do? Hand it off to the rest of the FBI? That isn't who you are. Especially not when there is a woman's life at stake."

Maya wanted to tell him that he was wrong, that he didn't know what he was talking about. But the truth was that this man, this killer, knew her about as well as anyone did.

That didn't mean that Maya had to admit it, though.

"If you don't have anything else to tell me, I don't have any reason to stay here," Maya said.

She got up, taking the postcard, half-hoping that Frank might tell her something simply to keep her there. Instead, he laughed.

"A transparent ploy, Maya. Besides, I'm sure we'll be seeing one another soon enough. Have fun in Ellonsea."

"I haven't decided that I'm going yet."

"You have, Maya, even if you won't admit it to yourself."

Maya left the interrogation room, grateful to be out of there. Being in a room with Frank brought too many bad memories. Had she gotten anything out of her trip here?

Not much, but there *had* been the confirmation that this was an unsolved case, that Maya wouldn't be wasting her time hunting for a second killer when the Moonlight Killer was truly responsible.

That was important, because it meant that she wasn't walking into something that couldn't be solved, but Maya was angry by how much Frank had held back. He could have told her who was holding Lucy or who was responsible for the murder. Instead, he was treating it like another of his games.

The question was, was it a game Maya was going to play? Of course it was. She didn't have a choice if Lucy was going to live.

CHAPTER NINE

Maya paced her living room, trying to make a decision about what to do next.

The postcard was on the room's coffee table, sitting there in invitation, or accusation, Maya wasn't sure which, only that it was there, and it wasn't going away.

She had spent the last hour going over everything she knew about the Ellonsea case in her head. She'd read through the files on her computer, trying to discover more, to find something that she hadn't paid attention to. The problem was that Maya had already been through the files a hundred times.

Rose Kallen had been thirty-one years old, working as the overnight clerk in a shipping yard on the night of the full moon when she'd died.

The killer had been neat. There hadn't been any DNA or fibers left behind at the scene. It didn't help that the murder had taken place in the open air, where such things quickly washed away.

It was a mystery, the kind that caught Maya's attention, that it was almost impossible to look past.

But did she really want to dive headfirst into another serial killer case? Maya had already caught one of the most notorious killers in recent history. Did she really want to risk her life again by jumping into something like this alone?

Maya sat there, trying to think. She knew what she ought to do. She *ought* to take the postcard straight to her colleagues in the FBI. She ought to call Agent Swift, since she'd been the one previously running the Moonlight Killer taskforce, and this connected to one of the crimes he'd been convicted of.

Maya knew that she ought to do all of that. At the very least, she should head out to the field office she worked at and get the aid of a couple of the junior agents there.

But Maya knew what was likely to happen then. The same thing that had happened all the other times with the Moonlight Killer: the FBI would go chasing after the kidnapper rather than trying to help her solve the case. The kidnapper had told her what would happen if she did that.

There was also a part of Maya that couldn't resist the challenge. She had always been drawn to the hunt, to unraveling the twisted mind of a killer. It was why she had joined the FBI, and why she had excelled in Military Intelligence before that. Maya had a knack for seeing patterns where others couldn't, for finding the needle in the haystack.

And if there was a woman's life at stake, Maya couldn't just sit around and wait for someone else to solve the case.

It would *be* someone else, too. If Maya went to her superiors with this, she had no doubt that they would assign someone else to the case, given that she mostly worked a desk these days, while other agents were out in the field. She guessed that someone like Swift might want a different agent on the case, too, someone who didn't have the baggage that came with Maya's hunt for the Moonlight Killer.

Then there was what was written on the postcard. The kidnapper claimed that if Maya went to the FBI or the police, if they started hunting for him, then Lucy would die.

Maya had experience with how the FBI would react to this kind of kidnapping. Her former boss, Harris, had tried to hunt down the Moonlight Killer from the moment that he'd kidnapped Megan and eleven other women. He'd conducted raids based on the slenderest evidence, focusing on getting the kidnapped women back rather than on solving the cases that Maya was set.

What if it was the same now? Maya knew that if she went to the FBI, they would do everything in their power to rescue Lucy, but they might not be able to do it in time. Time was of the essence in kidnapping cases, and even if Maya trusted her colleagues' abilities, she wasn't sure she could trust their methods.

Maya took a deep breath and picked up the postcard. She read it over again, feeling the weight of the words: *You have until midnight, three days from now.*

Three days, and Maya was still in DC, trying to decide if she should even take the case or hand it over to her colleagues.

If she couldn't trust the rest of the FBI on this case, could she at least get help from Marco?

She loved him, and when it had come to the previous cold cases Maya had been forced to work, they had worked together closely, spending long nights chasing leads, analyzing evidence and brainstorming theories. He was one of the few people she trusted completely in the bureau. Maya had no doubt that if she called him, he would want to help.

Maya wondered if Marco would be willing to help her again. She knew he was out in the field, but maybe he would be able to lend a hand, or at least offer some advice.

Maya picked up her phone and got ready to dial his number. Any other time, she would have done it without thinking. This was the man she was engaged to marry, after all, not to mention her former partner in so many similar cases.

Three things stopped Maya from calling him. The first was that Marco was out in the field somewhere, probably working undercover. Calling him now might not get through to him, might distract him while he was working, might even put him in danger. Certainly, Maya couldn't just demand that he come back, that he drop everything to come help her in this.

Especially when Maya wasn't even sure that he would approve of what she was doing. That was the second reason that Maya didn't call Marco.

He obviously agreed with Megan that she'd been obsessing about the idea that there were three unsolved cases. The fact that she had proof of that now would only make that worse, not better. He would see this as Maya getting drawn back in. He would be worried about the danger it would put her in.

The third reason was that Maya was sure that Marco would want to do all of this by the book. He was an agent now, he would have to. He would call it in, insist that they got backup. If he didn't... well, that would put him in a difficult position. The bureau would probably see it as him putting his fiance ahead of his duty to the FBI.

Maya didn't want to put him in that position. She didn't want to make Marco choose, so she put her phone down. She closed her eyes and took a deep breath. Maya knew that she had to make a decision and make it soon.

She couldn't just sit around and let Lucy be kidnapped without doing anything. Maya's instincts as an FBI agent were screaming at her to take action, to do something, anything, to save the woman's life. Maya knew that she was the only one who could solve this case. She had done it before, and she could do it again.

She knew what she had to do, even if it went against everything she had been taught in the FBI.

Maya had to go to Ellonsea and hunt for the killer herself. She had to do this on her own, without backup. The kidnapper had said that she needed to be the one to solve this, and so she would.

Maya started to hurry through the house, packing a bag. What did it say about how settled her life had become now that she no longer had a go bag ready for the moment when the next case came along? Her life had slowed down, become a lot safer. She did *paperwork* now.

For the first time in what felt like months, Maya felt as though the world was speeding up around her. She felt alive again. What did it say about her that she was faced with a cold case, about to go off to a town along the coast, trying to crack a case before a woman was killed, and it made her feel better than she had in a long time?

That was another reason Maya had to be the one to do this.

She called in sick to work. Perhaps they would think that she needed the time off after the funeral, if they questioned it at all. Maya sent a message to Marco, hoping that he wouldn't worry.

I have to go away for a few days. A bit of a family emergency. Cousin Barney's sick.

Maya added the last detail to make it less likely that Marco would question it, even though she didn't have a Cousin Barney. She didn't like lying to him like that, but she didn't want him to worry, and in any case, it was kind of true. She was researching one of the old cases.

It was just that if she didn't find an answer, Lucy Barnet was going to die.

CHAPTER TEN

For the second time in her life, Lucy was sitting in a cage. A cage that was just one of several, dotted around an open space that looked like some kind of basement, or warehouse or something.

She was alone with her terror there, trying to make sense of what had happened. A part of her insisted that it knew what had happened, that *he* had taken her again. Yet Lucy knew that Michael Hanratty couldn't have done it. That he hadn't done it.

So much was the same here: the fact that she'd been abducted so smoothly; the fact that there were the multiple cages here; the fact that it was her he'd taken rather than someone else. Lucy had no doubt that it was connected to what had happened before.

Yet there were also things that were different. The Moonlight Killer had let her and the others out of their cages to wander his bunker freely. Lucy's captor had shown no sign of letting her out yet. He'd let her keep her clothes. He seemed to have set up communications devices here, in the main room he was holding her in.

And, of course, he'd let Lucy see his face.

He walked in now, wearing cargo pants and a dark sweater. He wasn't wearing a mask, wasn't wearing gloves, as though it didn't matter if Lucy was able to identify him.

That was a terrifying thought in itself. The Moonlight Killer had been careful to protect his identity, because it turned out that he'd meant it about releasing his hostages when Agent Gray succeeded.

If this one didn't mind Lucy seeing his face, did that mean that he didn't plan to let her go? Did that mean that Lucy was going to have to escape by herself?

He came over to the cage and looked at Lucy like she was nothing.

"You're not the Moonlight Killer," Lucy said.

He shrugged. "Do I need to be?"

"Why are you doing this?" Lucy asked. Once, she would have been paralyzed by terror. She was still terrified, but she'd learned that she had to be strong. She had to keep some hope.

"Because his work isn't finished," her captor said. "Maya Gray cheated. *You* cheated, the moment you escaped. The rules were clear."

"So, you're trying to finish the Moonlight Killer's work?" Lucy asked, barely able to understand why anyone would want to do that.

"It needs to happen. Exactly the way he set it out. The purity of his work must be preserved. The truth must be told about it!"

The man sounded like a fanatic when he said that, or perhaps a madman. Neither one gave Lucy any confidence.

"Already, I've sent Maya Gray the task that she must perform," her captor said. He went over to his banks of screens. He typed for a moment or two, and a countdown came up on the screen.

"Less than three days now. If Agent Gray finds the truth, you get to go free. If she fails, then... well, then you'll die the way you should have a year ago."

CHAPTER ELEVEN

Maya wanted to be ready when she got to Ellonsea.

It was only a short flight over to Ellonsea, but Maya used it to make sure that she had all the details of the case. She'd read through the files on the fifteen murders the Moonlight Killer had been convicted of so many times now that she was pretty sure she knew the details by heart, but Maya wanted to focus in on Rose Kallen's murder. That was what mattered now.

No, what mattered was solving it before the deadline she'd been given. Trying to save Lucy from the fate that awaited her otherwise.

That might await her even if Maya succeeded. Lucy hadn't been taken by the Moonlight Killer, but by a copycat. Maya had no way of knowing if he would react in the same ways, if he would keep his word about releasing her when Maya succeeded.

She had to believe that she would succeed in this, even though she was alone now, without even Marco to back her up.

It was like being back on the first case the Moonlight Killer had sent her, looking into the murder of Anne Postmartin. Maya had gone out on it alone, not knowing for sure if she could find an answer in time, not knowing if succeeding really would lead to the release of a hostage. But she'd still had to take the chance because the alternative was worse.

Maya got a clear view of the town as her plane came around to land at a small airport a little way outside it. It hugged the Atlantic coast like a limpet, with rows of pastel-colored houses lining the shore. She couldn't help but think that it was a beautiful place, even with the heavy weight of the case on her shoulders.

Maya couldn't help but feel a sense of unease as she looked down at the town below. She knew that this was the place where Rose Kallen had died and that there was a killer on the loose. One who had killed more than one person if Hanratty had been telling her the truth.

As she stepped off the plane and into the airport terminal, she took a deep breath and tried to push aside her apprehension. She had a job to do, and it was one that she had to treat with the utmost seriousness.

There was no one waiting for Maya when she landed, which made a change from a lot of the cases she'd worked. She hadn't let the local cops know that she was coming. She hadn't made any arrangements with the closest FBI field office.

The truth was that Maya couldn't afford that kind of attention on this, both because it might spook the kidnapper into killing Lucy, and because it would draw attention to the way Maya was conducting this investigation outside of the usual chain of command. Maya was at a level where she had some freedom to pick up cases that came across her desk, but she still knew that her superiors wouldn't see it that way. She would be on her own for this case.

Maya made her way to the car rental desk, where she picked up a small, nondescript sedan. She had to blend in, not draw attention to herself. Maya would have to remember that this was a civilian car without hidden lights or a siren. It wasn't the kind of thing she could afford to have some high-speed chase in.

Maya threw her bag in the trunk and set off in the direction of the shipping office where Rose Kallen had worked as an overnight clerk. It was already well into the afternoon, and Maya didn't want to waste time finding a motel until she needed to. When she only had a couple more days on this case, she wanted to make some progress quickly.

Ellonsea Global Shipping proved to be a lot less grand than its name suggested. The offices were in a small, shabby building down near the docks, close enough that the smell of the sea air and the diesel from the closest boats filled Maya's nostrils. The building looked like it had been converted from an old warehouse, and there was still a storage space underneath, with the offices on an upper floor.

Maya parked the car and got out, her eyes scanning the area as she tried to understand where the murder had taken place, mentally fitting the image in front of her against the crime scene photographs taken at the time.

The office where Rose Kallen had worked would be up there, and *that* would be the fire escape balcony where she'd been found the next morning, strangled with a length of rope that had been left behind at the scene. There had been no prints or DNA to work with, no obvious physical clues. Maya would have to find answers here another way.

It was a way that couldn't involve identifying herself as an FBI agent if she could avoid it. The local cops would soon hear about an FBI agent in town, and presumably, so would Maya's superiors. She needed to do this another way. Maya needed to be undercover for this one, the same way Marco would be with whatever investigation he was working on right then.

Thankfully, Maya had exactly the kind of cover story that might work. One with enough truth in it that there wouldn't be many chances of being caught out on the details.

Maya headed over to the building, pulling her jacket tighter around her. The chill from the Atlantic wind made her shiver, but she ignored it, focusing on the task at hand.

She walked into the building, feeling tension building inside her. Maya knew that she had to be careful, that she couldn't let anyone know who she really was. She had to play the part of a writer looking into the Moonlight Killer's old murders, and she had to do it convincingly.

Maya walked up to the front desk, where a young woman in her mid-twenties was typing away on a computer. She had blonde hair and was wearing a cream sweater along with a dark skirt. She looked up as Maya approached.

"Hi there," Maya said, flashing a warm smile, hoping that enough confidence would see her through this. "I'm sorry to bother you, but I was wondering if you could point me in the direction of Rose Kallen's old office?"

The woman looked at Maya quizzically for a moment, and then frowned.

"Why do you want to be there? Who are you, anyway?"

This was the last moment where Maya could just come clean and flash her badge, but she was still certain that would cause more trouble than it solved.

"My name's Maya. I'm... look, I'm writing a book, all about the Moonlight Killer murders. I know that can be a little grizzly for some people, though."

"Oh no," the young woman said. "It's fascinating. I was listening to a podcast just the other day looking into what his motivations might have been."

She seemed excited by it all. A part of Maya wanted to say that Hanratty's motives had probably been nothing more than a series of dark urges he'd had since childhood, and that Maya had nearly been killed stopping him, but she knew that she couldn't.

"So, is there any chance that I could get to see the office?" Maya asked.

“Well, it’s obviously still in use, but I guess… maybe. I probably shouldn’t.”

“If you do, I’ll make sure that you get a special mention in the book when it comes out,” Maya offered. It was the best thing she had to bargain with right then.

The receptionist looked thoughtful for a few seconds.

"Okay," the receptionist said, at last. "If I show you up, it should be fine. I'm Hannah."

She offered Maya her hand, and Maya shook it. Hannah led her up to the shipping office, which was quite large. Rows of filing cabinets lined the walls, and stacks of papers cluttered the desks. Maya looked around, trying to take in as much as she could without looking too suspicious. The walls were a dull gray, with a few posters advertising shipping services on them, and a curious clock on one wall had the numbers 1-5 going up one side and down the other. A small window on one side of the room overlooked the docks below, letting anyone in there see the ships arriving.

There was a clerk working in the office. He was a middle-aged man with graying hair and a thick mustache, and he looked up at Maya and Hannah as they entered.

"Hey there, what can I do for you ladies?" he asked, his tone friendly.

Hannah smiled. "Thomas, this is Maya, she's a writer doing a book on the Moonlight Killer. She wanted to take a look at Rose Kallen's old office."

The clerk's expression turned serious. "Oh yeah, poor Rose. That was a terrible thing that happened to her."

Maya nodded, trying to appear sympathetic. "Yes, it's a tragedy. I don't want to intrude. I just wanted to see if I could learn more about what happened to her by coming here."

"That's..." Thomas didn't look happy that Maya was asking questions, which made her worry that she might have to either leave or announce herself as an FBI agent to get answers.

Thankfully, Hannah intervened.

"Thomas, it's okay. Let's just help her, right? She has a book to write, and I bet this won't take long. Don't you want her to get the facts right in her book?"

Thomas still looked a little doubtful, but he eventually nodded.

"All right," he said. "I guess it can't do any more harm. What do you want to know?"

"Did you know Rose Kallen?" Maya asked.

"Sure," Thomas said. "She was the overnight clerk, while I was here in the day. She was a nice lady, always had a smile on her face. It was a real shock when we found out what happened to her."

Maya nodded, trying to show empathy.

"I can imagine. Can you tell me anything about what happened to her? I've looked at some of the official descriptions of it all, but those always seem to miss out the details."

Thomas shrugged. "There's not a lot to tell. I was the one who found her that morning when I came in to take over running the office. It was..."

Maya could see how much the moment haunted him just by looking at how pale he went as he struggled to find the words. Still, she knew that she had to keep going.

"I know this is hard, Thomas. You didn't see anything unusual then, did you? Anything that the police didn't talk about?"

Thomas shrugged. "I don't know what you're looking for. All I saw was Rose and the rope that Hanratty guy used to kill her."

Of course, by now, everyone knew that Frank had been found guilty. Maya would have to work around that.

"Obviously, we've all heard about the Moonlight Killer being caught," she said. "But at the time, do you remember what you were thinking? Did anyone strike you as a likely suspect? Do you know if she had any enemies, or if there was anyone who might have wanted to harm her?"

Thomas looked thoughtful for a moment. "I can't say that I know of anyone who would want to hurt her. She mostly kept to herself and didn't seem to have any enemies that I know of."

Maya made a mental note of this, and then asked, "Can you tell me anything about the night that she was killed? Was there anything unusual about the shipping office that night?"

Thomas shook his head. "No, not that I remember. It was a quiet night like any other. Rose was here doing her job, and I assume Frank Hanratty came in and did what he did."

Maya nodded, trying to hide her disappointment. She had hoped for some new information that would help her in her investigation.

"Thank you for your time, Thomas. I really appreciate it," she said, turning to leave. "Hannah, thank you for showing me up here."

Maya went to leave. She'd struck out here, getting nothing that wasn't in the files already. She would need to try elsewhere.

Maybe Rose's family would be able to tell her more.

CHAPTER TWELVE

Maya took the address for Rose's sister, Aisling, from the files. She just hoped that it was up to date because she didn't want to have to dig around too much officially to find the information. She couldn't afford the extra attention on her actions.

Aisling Kallen lived in a small house on the outskirts of Ellonsea, at the end of a cul-de-sac. Its only claim to grandeur was a small porch with two wooden chairs, the paint chipped and the wood worn. The grass was overgrown, and the trees were beginning to obscure the house.

As Maya pulled up to the house, she knew that this wouldn't be easy. Working cold cases had shown her that talking to family members could be emotional and difficult because they often didn't want someone trying to dig up the past. It was hard enough persuading them to open up, even with the aid of her FBI credentials. As the writer she was pretending to be, it might prove even more difficult, but she had to try.

Maya took a deep breath and got out of the car, going up to the house. She knocked on the door, preparing herself for what might happen next, how hard the next few minutes might be.

A woman who had to be Aisling Kallen opened the door. She was in her early thirties, with striking features and a haunted look in her eyes. Maya could tell that Rose's death had affected her deeply.

"Can I help you?" Aisling asked, suspicion in her voice.

"Hello, Ms. Kallen," Maya said, offering a warm smile. "My name is Maya. I'm a writer. I'm currently writing a book on the Moonlight Killer's murders."

"So you thought you'd come and pump me for information?" Aisling snapped. "For some book that's going to spend all its time glorifying a man who murdered my sister?"

Maya shook her head. She could understand Aisling's anger, but she wanted to find a way to get information from her that wouldn't blow Maya's cover story and lead to too many complications with the FBI.

She didn't want another FBI investigation where the lead agent might try to go after the kidnapper rather than letting Maya solve the murder.

Thankfully, there was one thing Maya could say that was absolutely true.

"The *last* thing I want to do is glorify Hanratty. I know, probably as well as anyone, just how evil he is. And how dangerous. I... I've spoken to all the women he kidnapped. The ones he tried to use to get the FBI to investigate murders he didn't commit that were ascribed to him."

There must have been something about the way Maya said it that conveyed the weight of her hatred for Frank after everything he'd done. Or maybe just the pain that she'd felt at having her sister Megan taken captive by the serial killer.

"You sound like it's more than that," Aisling said.

"I have some personal connections to all of this," Maya said, although she couldn't say what those were without giving away the whole truth. "And I'm interested in the truth."

"Even so," Aisling said. "I'm not sure that I want to get dragged into some tell-all book about a man who took my sister from me."

"Michael Francis Hanratty claims that your sister's case was one of the ones he would have tried to make the FBI look into, if they hadn't caught him," Maya said. "He claims he didn't do it."

"How do you know that?" Aisling asked, looking both shocked and disbelieving.

Maya knew that there was only one thing to say to that. "Because I spoke to him. Can I come inside, Aisling?"

Aisling hesitated for a moment before stepping back and allowing Maya inside.

As they made their way to the living room, Maya took a quick glance around the house. It was a modest living space, but it was tidy and well-kept. It seemed like Aisling had put a lot of effort into making it a cozy home for herself.

Maya sat down on the couch, crossing her legs and looking up at Aisling.

"Tell me more about this conversation you had with Hanratty," Aisling said, her eyes fixed on Maya. "Aren't prisons full of people who claim that they never did the things they were convicted of?"

"That's the thing," Maya said. "He's happy to admit that he's killed other people. *This* murder, though, he claims wasn't him. And if that's true..."

She left that hanging for a second or two to let the implications sink in for Aisling.

"That would mean that someone else killed my sister," she said. "That her killer is still out there somewhere. No, that can't... I've only just started to piece my life back together after what happened to Rose."

"I know it's hard," Maya said, sympathetically. "I know that me coming here like this disrupts the closure that you thought you had when Hanratty was convicted."

"Then why come?" Aisling snapped at her.

"Because if Rose's real killer is still out there, they deserve to be found. We should know the real truth about what happened, not a comfortable fiction that lets a killer walk free."

Aisling hesitated for several seconds. It seemed to Maya as if she were wrestling with that, wishing that Maya hadn't come over to her home to tell her this. Finally, though, she nodded.

"You're right. I'd rather know the truth about what happened, no matter how hard it is. And you think you can find that truth?"

Maya nodded. "I hope so, at least."

"Even though you're just a writer? Shouldn't you go to the police or something? The FBI?"

"I don't know if the police would believe me," Maya said. "And no law enforcement agency will reopen a case like this without some kind of evidence. As far as they're concerned, this case is closed, and the right man is in prison."

"Then what can you do?" Aisling asked, her voice tinged with desperation.

"I can investigate," Maya said simply. "I can talk to people, look for clues, and try to piece together what really happened to your sister. And if I find something, I can bring it to the authorities. Maybe then they'll be willing to reopen the case."

Aisling nodded slowly. "Okay. I'll help you however I can. But I don't know what good I'll be. I already told the police everything I knew at the time. But I'll answer any questions you have."

"Why don't you start by telling me what Rose was like?" Maya said. There was an art to asking questions in cold cases. She needed to start by getting Aisling to think back, to make sure that her memory of the time was clear.

Aisling took a deep breath and began to speak. "Rose was the best thing that ever happened to me. We were sisters, but we were also best friends. She was funny, kind and always knew how to make me smile. She loved to sing and dance. She was in the church choir, and whenever she sang, it was like the whole world lit up. Everyone loved her. She had this infectious energy that just drew people in. She was also incredibly smart. She could have been anything she wanted, but college was never an option for us. She took jobs around the town until she got married. After the divorce, she ended up working at the shipping office."

"As the overnight clerk?" Maya said, starting to make careful notes in a small notebook.

Aisling nodded. "Yes, she worked the overnight shift. I remember her coming home in the morning, tired but always with a smile on her face. It wasn't until she died that I found out she was working that shift because it paid more. She was trying to save up money to get out of Ellonsea, to build a new life for herself."

A woman on the cusp of change. It had been one of the reasons that even Maya hadn't been able to tell the case apart from the Moonlight Killer's true kills.

"I know the police settled on this being a Moonlight Killer case pretty quickly," Maya said. "But do you remember them focusing on anything else before that? Did they ever mention anything to you, or did you hear anything around town about what was going on?"

"Most of the rumors were about the Moonlight Killer from the start," Aisling said. "It all seemed so obvious at the time. A woman strangled under the full moon? It had to be him, right?"

"So the police never looked in any other directions that you know about?" Maya asked.

"There was one thing," Aisling said. "There were some people that night who said they saw my sister with a man down on the docks, earlier that night."

"Did they have any idea who?" Maya asked, making a note of it.

Aisling shook her head. "No one seems to have seen his face. I know the police were frustrated by it because they guessed he would have been the last person to see her alive. Then, I think they thought that he must have been the Moonlight Killer."

Maya could imagine the police's frustration with that. They must have thought that if they could only find a witness who had a clear view, they would get a description of the Moonlight Killer. Well, it might not have been Frank, but it was still possible that people *had* seen Rose with whoever killed her.

Maya turned her attention to a more general question. "Did Rose have any enemies? Had she argued with anyone? Was there anyone who might have wanted to hurt her?"

For a moment, she thought that Aisling would say no, the way most people did at this point. The majority of people had a hard time believing that anyone would want to hurt their loved ones.

Instead, Aisling nodded. "That no good ex-husband of hers."

"You mentioned him before," Maya said. "What can you tell me about him?"

Aisling's expression turned sour. "His name is Jack. Jack Hemling. He and Rose were married for a little over four years before they divorced. He was a cheating scumbag, and I'm pretty sure he was abusive to her, both physically and emotionally. She tried to leave him several times, but he always managed to talk her back into staying."

Maya furrowed her brow in concern. "Did Rose ever report him to the police?"

"No," Aisling said, shaking her head. "She didn't want to believe that he was capable of hurting her, I think. And she was afraid of what he would do if he found out she had gone to the police."

All of which made him sound like exactly the kind of man who might want to hurt his wife after they'd divorced.

Aisling kept going. "Finally, she got the courage to leave him, but he never stopped harassing her. He kept calling and showing up at her job. She even had to get a restraining order against him."

Maya's mind raced. Could it be that Jack was the man seen with Rose on the docks? Could he have followed her and killed her after she left? Those were just conjectures, but they were worth investigating.

One thing didn't make sense.

"If he was like that, why didn't the police look into him at the time?"

"They said they did," Aisling said. "He claimed to have an alibi, said he was out of town, or something. But they were all so set on it being the Moonlight Killer by then, from what I heard, they didn't even get around to checking the alibi properly."

Which meant that there was a chance that he didn't have an alibi at all. Maya would have to check how closely the local cops had checked the alibi.

Of course, to do that, she was going to have to go talk to the Ellonsea PD.

CHAPTER THIRTEEN

Maya stood outside the Ellonsea PD, not sure what she should do next.

It was a three-story building in the middle of the town, square and weathered until it looked almost like a boulder squatting there among the brightly painted buildings around it. Police vehicles clustered around the base of the building, ready to go out on calls at a moment's notice.

The big question when it came to talking to the local PD was how much Maya should tell them, about herself, and about the case she was working. Should she go in there with the same story that she'd been using through the rest of the town, about being a writer looking into the case for her book, rather than being an FBI agent?

Maya knew that she had to play it that way. If she went in with the truth, there would be too much of a chance of it all getting back to the FBI, and the investigation escalating to the point where the kidnapper killed Lucy Barnet. He'd told her that he would kill Lucy if the FBI tried to find him, and if they knew about what was going on, there was a chance that was exactly what they would do.

Maya took a deep breath, reminding herself that she was a skilled agent. She could handle this small piece of undercover work. She made her way into the building, looking around at the interior of the police department, trying to understand some of the ways things worked there.

The main lobby of the police department was painted a pale blue. A woman at a desk sat in the center of the room, checking people in. The counter behind her was buried under stacks of papers and folders.

Lines of desks stood further back in a bullpen, separated by narrow aisles, like a factory floor. The desks were old, battered and some marked with the scars of years of use. The air smelled of stale coffee and body odor.

The lobby was almost deserted, with only a few officers milling around behind the front desk. Maya walked up to the desk, her heart pounding in her chest.

"Excuse me," she said, trying to keep her voice steady. "I'm looking to speak to someone who worked on the Rose Kallen murder."

"And what's your interest in that?" the woman at the desk said.

"I'm a writer," Maya said smoothly, pulling out her notebook and holding it up for her to see. "I'm researching a book on the Moonlight Killer, looking at some of the cases he was convicted for."

The woman raised an eyebrow. "Do you have an appointment?"

Maya shook her head. "No, I'm afraid I didn't think that far ahead. I'm just passing through town and thought I'd stop in."

The woman looked at Maya skeptically for a moment before nodding. "Okay, hold on a minute."

She picked up the phone and made a call, speaking quietly into the receiver.

"Wait here," she said to Maya, gesturing to a chair in the lobby. Maya sat there, wondering if she was going to get to talk to one of the detectives working on the case.

She had to sit there for long minutes, to the extent that she suspected the police were ignoring her, waiting for her to go away.

Finally, an older man in a suit came out, heading for Maya. He was tall and carried himself well, with a bit of a stoop in the way he walked. He was an older man with silver hair and piercing blue eyes. His suit was dark blue and tattered at the edges, like it had been worn for decades on the job. His voice was like gravel, tumbling stones in a riverbed.

"You're the writer?" he said. "I'm Chief Dearing."

Maya nodded, jumping up from her seat and offering her hand. "Maya."

She deliberately left off her surname. She didn't want him searching for her that easily

He ignored her hand. "Tammy tells me that you're here asking questions about the Rose Kallen case?"

"That's right," Maya said.

"What questions?" Chief Dearing asked. "The case is closed, and the relevant information came out in the trial."

Maya wasn't sure how to get more out of him. She started off cautiously.

"I hoped that I could get more details about the investigations into the different cases from some of the people who were there," Maya said. "I want to go deeper than just the trial records."

"So you came to Ellonsea to talk to us without even calling ahead?" Chief Dearing asked. "You could have saved yourself a lot of time."

"Like I said to your receptionist, I was passing through the town and thought I'd stop in," Maya said. "I thought it would be better to speak to people who were on the ground, as it were."

Chief Dearing looked at her for a moment before nodding. "All right. What specifically are you looking for in the Kallen case? My department only investigated for a brief time before the FBI barged in to take over."

He sounded a little bitter about the FBI's involvement. Maybe Maya had made the right choice, not telling him that she was working with them.

"I'm looking at any alternative theories you may have had at the time," she said. "I heard that this crime is one that the Moonlight Killer isn't claiming as his."

"So you're trying to re-open the whole can of worms?" Chief Dearing said, suddenly sounding a lot less friendly. His eyes narrowed. "What? You're going to try to say that my department didn't do a good enough job? Is that the angle for this book of yours? Trying to tear down all the different investigations?"

"That's not it at all," Maya said. "I just heard that maybe Rose's ex-husband was a suspect for a while."

"Jack Hemling doesn't come into this," Chief Dearing said. "And I'm done answering questions. If all you're going to do is try to make out that there was something wrong with the Moonlight Killer's conviction, you're in the wrong place."

"I know he committed plenty of murders," Maya said, "but with this one, don't you think-"

"No, I don't," Chief Dearing said. "What I think is that you should leave my police department before I find something to arrest you for."

Maya cursed silently. She'd gone wrong somewhere with this approach. Maybe she'd been too pushy, trying to get information out of him.

She considered pulling her badge and doing things that way, but she suspected that it wouldn't help at this point. It was obvious that he didn't like the FBI, and he definitely wouldn't appreciate the subterfuge.

Maya's only option was to leave, heading back out into the parking lot and sitting in her rented sedan as she tried to work out what choices she had right then.

She could call all of this in, of course, turning it into an official investigation. There would be a lot of questions then, though, and Maya might even find herself pulled off the case. That would put Lucy Barnet in danger, so Maya couldn't afford to risk it.

Did she just ignore the police department instead, carrying on without any information they could give her? It seemed like the only option she had right then, and she had plenty of experience of working without local police support.

Maya was still considering how best to proceed when she saw a detective coming out of the police department, heading right for her car. Had Chief Dearing sent someone out to make sure that she'd gone?

The detective was an unremarkable man in a wrinkled suit with thinning hair and several days worth of stubble. The detective was tall, but thin, wiry. He might have been thirty or forty years old, but his face was still young, his eyes fixed on Maya.

He came up to the car and rapped on the driver's side window. Maya lowered it, expecting to be told that she had to move on.

"You're the writer?" the detective said. "The one who was asking about the Rose Kallen case?"

Maya nodded. "That's right. I'm just going. Your chief said he didn't want to talk to me."

"Oh, ignore him," the detective said. He held out a hand. "I'm Detective Kreese. I worked the Rose Kallen case."

"And you're prepared to talk to me?" Maya asked, barely able to believe it.

Detective Kreese nodded. "Just not here. Meet me down the street on the corner of Arnison and Fifth in five minutes."

He gestured to the street corner before walking away. Maya quickly started her car and drove to the designated spot, parking and waiting for the detective. It was getting into evening now, the light starting to fade a little.

It worried Maya a little, waiting like that. It seemed obvious that Detective Kreese didn't want to be seen talking to her, but there were plenty of other reasons why someone might not want to be seen. Maybe he wanted to threaten her, or even hurt her, for looking into this case.

If so, Maya would deal with it. It was worth the risk if she might find out something that would help in the case.

It was several long minutes before Detective Kreese came walking up to the car. He looked around before approaching the car and getting into the passenger seat.

"Sorry about that," he said, rubbing his hands together. "Dearing's not exactly fond of outsiders asking about his cases. But I figured if you're here, you must have a good reason."

Maya nodded, feeling a glimmer of hope. "I appreciate it. I'm just trying to get as much information as I can about the case. I think there might be more to it than what's been documented."

Detective Kreese looked at her for a few moments before nodding. "I understand. I've had my own suspicions about the case over the years. It was one that never quite sat right with me when we had to hand it over to the FBI as a Moonlight Killer case."

"Did you have other leads?" Maya asked.

"I always thought that the ex-husband was worth looking into," Detective Kreese said. Jack Hemling was a suspect for a while, you're right about that. But we couldn't find any concrete evidence against him, and the chief says that he had an alibi."

"What kind of alibi?" Maya asked.

Detective Kreese shrugged. "I think he was meant to be out of town. The chief was happy that it couldn't be him."

"So you checked the alibi out thoroughly?" Maya asked. That was the crucial question. If the alibi didn't check out, then maybe he worked as a suspect after all.

"I'm not sure," Detective Kreese admitted. "Once the FBI came in, we stopped looking into it all, and it's been a while since then. Look, do you really think that this might not be the Moonlight Killer?"

"I'm convinced of it," Maya said. "But I need to find more evidence before I can present it all to the authorities."

"Well, I wish you luck with that," Detective Kreese said. "Not that I can do much to help you. But if you get that evidence, maybe bring it to me. I'd like the chance to finish this one."

Maya nodded, although if she found the killer, she would be the one to arrest him. She waited for Detective Kreese to get out of the car, then drove away, trying to think.

He hadn't given her much, but he had confirmed that the suspicions about Jack Hemling were more than just in Aisling's head. His alibi was... well, how solid *was* it?

There was only one way to find out. Maya was going to have to ask him.

CHAPTER FOURTEEN

Maya sat outside Jack Hemling's house, trying to decide if it looked like the house of a killer, and what she should do if it did.

It was dark now, street lights shining down on the painted front of it, a pastel green that Maya wasn't sure that she would have chosen. It sat at the heart of a row of other brightly painted town houses, squashed together near the heart of the town.

Maya got out of the car, heading for the front door. She took a deep breath, trying to calm her nerves. This was a risk, going to the prime suspect's house alone like this. Especially when she But Maya was confident in her ability to handle herself.

She knocked on the door, waiting for a response. A few moments later, Jack Hemling opened the door. He was in his thirties, a shorter man, not quite as tall as Maya. He was well built, clearly a man accustomed to exercise and well-toned, his skin pale. He was wearing jeans and a dark t-shirt. He looked surprised to see her, but didn't say anything.

"Mr. Hemling, my name is Maya. I'm a writer, and I'm talking to people connected to the old Moonlight Killer murders."

"I'm not-"

"Your ex-wife was killed by the Moonlight Killer, wasn't she?" Maya said, trying to keep moving quickly.

Jack spread his hands. "Well, yes. Look, what do you want?"

"I thought that, since you would have known Rose better than anyone else, you might be able to tell me a bit more about her. May I come in?" Maya was already stepping forward as she said it.

Jack hesitated for a moment before nodding and stepping aside for Maya to enter. She brushed past him, taking in the sight of the living room. It was sparsely decorated, with only a few pieces of furniture and no personal touches. It was clear that Jack wasn't much of a decorator.

"Can I get you anything to drink?" Jack asked awkwardly, gesturing towards the kitchen.

"No, thank you," Maya said. She needed to stay alert and focused. "I just have a few questions about Rose."

Jack sat down in a chair, gesturing for Maya to take a seat on the couch opposite him. She sat down, pulling out her notebook and a pen.

"Can you tell me about your relationship with Rose?" Maya asked, trying to keep her tone neutral.

Jack shifted uncomfortably in his seat. "We were married for a few years, but things didn't work out. We got divorced."

"Why did you get divorced?" Maya pressed, watching his reaction carefully.

Jack's jaw clenched. "It wasn't working. We were fighting all the time."

"Did Rose ever mention anything about feeling unsafe or threatened?" Maya asked, getting to the heart of what she really wanted to know.

"No," Jack said quickly. "Why would she?"

"I talked to her sister, Aisling," Maya said.

Jack's expression darkened. "Her? You can't listen to anything that bitch says."

"Especially not about you?" Maya guessed.

There was real anger there in Jack's eyes then.

"What is this? Some kind of hit piece aimed at me? Are you some friend of Aisling's?"

"I told you, I'm writing a book," Maya said. "I talked to her because she's Rose's closest surviving family member, and I'm talking to you because... well, because of some of the things Aisling said."

"Let me guess," Jack said, standing up so that he was looming over Maya. "Abusive husband. Violent man. All that bullshit."

"Would you mind sitting down, Mr. Hemling?" Maya said. It was obviously a tactic to try to intimidate her. It would have worked better if she hadn't faced down serial killers and psychopaths.

"You're going to try to tell me what to do in my own home?" Jack said, the anger obviously still there.

Maya could believe the accusations that he'd been abusive in that moment. It was obvious that Jack Hemling had a temper, one that felt as though it could spill over into violence at any moment.

"I'm not telling, I'm asking," Maya said, standing up. "It's obvious that you could tell me a lot that might help with my book, and I'm sorry if my questions are making you uncomfortable, but I need to ask them."

"Really?" Jack said. "You need to insult me by asking whether I abused my wife?"

"I haven't asked that," Maya said. She hadn't, not outright.

"No, but it's obvious you want to," Jack snapped. "You keep hinting at it. What are you even doing here now? How much work does it take to find out a bit about some woman who got herself strangled by a serial killer?"

Some woman? Maya thought. This was Jack's former wife, and he was dismissing her as if she were nothing.

Maya decided to reveal a little more about the reason for her visit.

"I'm here because the Moonlight Killer is claiming that he didn't commit this murder," Maya said.

She saw Jack's eyes widen at that. "What? That's impossible. He killed Rose, I know it."

"You know it?"

"It... it's obvious, isn't it? It doesn't matter what he says, he was found guilty."

"Because the police and the FBI are infallible?" Maya countered. "Didn't the police look at *you* for the murder until the FBI came in?"

She hoped that she'd found a way into what she really wanted to know that might get Jack to talk. If she could make this into him and her versus the police, he might see her as the kind of person he could confide in.

Jack gave Maya another angry look. "That was a long time ago. They couldn't prove anything. I didn't kill Rose," he said through gritted teeth. "And I don't appreciate you insinuating that I did."

"I'm not saying you did," Maya said calmly. "I just want to get to the truth. And the truth is, the Moonlight Killer has no reason to lie about this one case."

of Rose's murder."

"So what? That doesn't mean anything."

"It means that someone else could have killed her. Someone who knew her well."

Jack scoffed. "And you think that's me? You're barking up the wrong tree, lady. I loved Rose. I couldn't have hurt her."

"I'm not accusing you of anything," Maya said. "I just want to know everything that happened. It couldn't be you, right? You had an alibi. What was it again?"

Maya had her pen poised to note it down. If she could get Jack to commit to something, then she could check that alibi and find out whether it held up.

"I was out of town," Jack said.

"Where?" Maya asked.

"What's it to you?" Jack demanded, the anger back again. "What are you trying to do, make it look like I'm the killer here? Is that what this is? Is that your angle? You're going to go through all the Moonlight Killer's cases trying to find fall guys to pin things on?"

"I'm just trying to find the truth," Maya said.

"The truth, or some lie that suits you? Like her? Like Rose, saying all those things about me? I bet you're just like her. So tough, when there aren't any consequences."

Jack started towards Maya. She gave ground, realizing that this had gone too far. He was too close, and she could smell the alcohol on his breath, realizing too late that he'd been drinking. That made the situation more dangerous, harder to control, especially with someone who had already shown signs of violence.

Maya considered her options. She could try to get out of there, keeping her cover intact. If she did that, though, she might never get an answer when it came to the question of Jack's alibi. She wouldn't have anything definite that she could check, and the more time she spent around Jack, the greater her suspicions grew.

Maya flashed her badge instead. She was fairly confident that a man like Jack wouldn't be quick to go to the local police. "Think very carefully, Jack. My full name is Agent Maya Gray, of the FBI."

Jack just laughed. "Oh, so now you're pretending to be that agent who caught the Moonlight Killer? Nice try, bitch. I'm going to enjoy teaching you a lesson."

Maya hadn't considered the possibility that he might not even believe her. That was the problem with going undercover like this: it was harder to regain the authority that came from her position as a federal agent.

Jack lunged at Maya, his hands reaching for her throat. Maya was ready for him. She side-stepped his grab, turning so that she could put her shoulder into him and push him. As they grappled, she heard the sound of breaking glass, and then they hit the wall.

Maya took the opportunity to get her arms around Jack's neck and start pulling him to the floor. As they went down, Jack grabbed a hold of a lamp and swung it at her.

In the movies, Maya knew, people got up from much worse than a lamp to the head. In real life, it would be something else entirely. Maya blocked the blow, twisting the lamp out of Jack's hands, but then Jack was on her, his hands grabbing her throat, squeezing.

"You fucking bitch. I've got twenty eyewitnesses that put me well away from Ellonsea the night that woman got herself killed."

Maya bridged and rolled, coming up on top of Jack then. She managed to break his grip, grabbing Jack's arm and twisting. He snarled and fought, but Maya managed to force him to turn belly down. She got out her handcuffs, restraining his arms behind his back.

Maya sat there with her weight on him for several seconds, trying to catch her breath. Jack might be shorter than her, but he was stronger, and it took an effort to hold him down.

"Like I said, Jack," Maya said. "Agent Gray, FBI. And you just attacked me. Do you want me to drag you back to a field office and get you charged with assaulting a federal agent?"

Jack still struggled for a second or two, but then he went still.

Maya got to her feet, grabbing Jack by the arm and pulling him up. "How much have you had to drink today?"

"That's none of your business." Jack started to try and turn around, but Maya's hold on his arm kept him facing away from her.

"No, but what *is* my business is the part where you were an abusive husband, where Rose got away from you and you couldn't stand that."

"I didn't kill her," Jack said. "Like I said, I had an alibi."

"*What* alibi?" Maya demanded. "No more games, Jack. Either you tell me, or I drag you to the nearest FBI office tonight."

"I was out of town, at a hotel," Jack said. "It was... I'd gone there on a trip, met a woman. It didn't last. I can give you the name of the hotel. I checked in under my own name."

"Do that," Maya said.

"It was the Featherbed Hotel, up the coast. I still have the number for it."

"I can find it," Maya said. She looked up the number, taking the time to check how far away the hotel was. Too far for Jack to have driven back to murder his wife easily if he'd been there. She put in a call to the hotel. As she waited for someone to answer, Maya kept a tight grip on Jack's arm. He was seething with anger, still struggling to break free.

"Featherbed Hotel, how can I assist you?" The voice on the other end of the line was cheerful, professional.

"Yes, this is Agent Maya Gray of the FBI. I need to know if a man by the name of Jack Hemling was at your hotel on the night of July 12th."

That was the night Rose had died.

"Yes, we do have a record of a Jack Hemling checking in on the 10th of July," the receptionist said. "He was with us until the 13th."

"I don't suppose there's any chance that he left the hotel early on the 12th and didn't get back until the morning of the 13th?" Maya asked.

"No, I'd remember something like that," the receptionist said.

"Thank you," Maya said, and hung up. She felt frustration rising in her. She'd thought that this was such a good lead, yet this appeared to confirm Jack Hemling's alibi.

"I told you," Jack said, a note of triumph in his voice. "I didn't do anything."

Maya uncuffed his hands and pushed him away from her. A part of her still wanted to drag him in for attacking her, but that would make things too complicated on this case, telling the local cops exactly who she was.

Instead, she headed for the door. She'd hit a dead end. She needed to find a new approach.

CHAPTER FIFTEEN

Maya was still seething with the failure as she found a small motel, taking a room there. She didn't stay in it. Instead, she went out to get food from a small fish restaurant not far from the water. She looked out over the Atlantic, trying to find some kind of peace in the view, but that was hard when she knew that somewhere out there, a killer was still free, having persuaded the world that this was the Moonlight Killer's crime.

Maya hadn't felt as alone as she did right then in a long time. For so long now, she'd had Marco by her side on investigations. For almost all of the Moonlight Killer cases, he'd been there, both to back her up and to give her someone to bounce ideas off.

Maya looked around at her fellow diners, there in the restaurant. The clientele of the restaurant was a cross-section of tourists and locals, each looking out at the enticing view of the ocean. The tables were white linens, the chairs an almost sea foam green color.

Maya could see a family of five sitting there, the father in a suit, the mother in an off-the-shoulder business outfit, and three kids, one girl and two boys, all dressed in their finest clothes, all smiling, the oldest boy whispering to his younger sister, the two boys sharing a chocolate milkshake.

The smell of salt water and fresh fish hit her like a slap in the face as Maya opened the door when she finished her meal, heading outside. She was still thinking about Marco. These last few months, it had been so easy for the two of them to take one another for granted. So easy to let things drift, when their lives were going in such different directions.

Maya missed him, even though they'd only been apart for a day. It felt like longer, simply because of how much time she spent at the office and he spent out in the field. She missed him as a fiance, as a friend, but also as a partner who could help her work out the truth in often complex cases, where the reality of what had happened was hidden after months or years since the killings.

The thought was enough to make Maya reach for her phone, calling Marco as she stared out at the ocean. If there was anyone she could tell the truth to about all this, anyone she should have told the truth to from the start, it was Marco. Maya hadn't wanted to put him in a difficult position professionally, by asking him to keep things from the rest of the FBI, but now she realized that she needed him. She needed to be able to talk this over with him if she was going to get to the truth of Rose Kallen's murder. And if she didn't... well, Lucy Barnet was going to die.

Of course, Marco's phone went straight through to voicemail, exactly the way Maya should have expected if he was in the middle of something undercover. He'd told her before the dangers that would follow if he had his phone on him.

"Hi, this is Marco, I can't come to the phone right now. Probably busy catching bad guys. Leave a message."

Maya thought about telling him all about everything that had happened, but there were some things that it was better not to try to explain in a message.

Especially not given the reminder that Marco might be in the middle of an undercover operation somewhere. He probably wouldn't get the message until he was finished, in any case, but still, it probably wasn't a good idea to burden him with the knowledge that a Moonlight Killer copycat was making her investigate a cold case.

"Hi, Marco, it... it's me," Maya said, struggling to keep the tension she felt out of her voice. There were limits to what she could say, especially in a message like this that someone else from the FBI might be monitoring. "I just wanted to check on how you are. I guess you're not done with your case yet. I'm still dealing with the family stuff."

That would have to be good enough for now. Maya hung up, got in her sedan and headed back to the motel.

She went into her room, trying to plan what she would do tomorrow. The trouble was that it was hard to come up with a plan when she'd already blown her best lead today. Yes, she could start again, look into other aspects of Rose Kallen's life, but somehow, it didn't feel as though the answer was there.

Maya sat on her bed, using her laptop to go through the files in case there was anything in them that she didn't already know. She added in her notes from today, adding in what Aisling and Jack had told her.

Maya was still struggling with it all when her phone rang. She snatched it up, assuming that it was Marco, but instead, Megan's name came up on the screen.

Maya felt a moment of apprehension. Megan hadn't spoken to her since Imogen's funeral. Marco had said that he would talk to her, but it hadn't seemed as though it had done much good. Now she was calling? Why?

Maya took a deep breath before answering the call. "Hey, Megan, what's up?" she asked, her voice as calm as she could make it.

"Maya, where are you?" Megan asked.

"I'm out on the east coast," Maya said.

"*Where* on the east coast?" Megan asked.

Maya knew that she couldn't simply tell her sister the truth about that, because then she would have to explain everything that was happening, and she didn't want to drag Megan back into all this. Megan had been the Moonlight Killer's captive, and she'd made it clear at the funeral that she wanted to do everything she could to forget about that time. The last thing she would want to hear was that Lucy Barnet had been kidnapped for a second time, or that Maya was solving cold cases for a psychopath again.

"That doesn't matter," Maya said. "It's just a work thing."

"You told Marco that it was a family thing," Megan pointed out. "You said it was some kind of family emergency."

"Wait, you and Marco are talking about me?" Maya said. Her sister and her fiance were talking about Maya behind her back.

Megan hesitated on the other end of the phone. "Of course I talk to him. He helped save my life as much as you, and he's going to be my brother-in-law. Besides, we're both worried about you.

"You don't need to be worried about me," Maya said, although that was probably a lie.

"I'm sorry, I didn't mean to overstep. But I tried calling you earlier and you didn't answer, and then I talked to Marco, and he said that you were on some kind of trip dealing with a family emergency. What family emergency, Maya? If something were going on with Mom, I'd have heard."

Maya's heart began to race, and she tried to keep her voice calm. "I just needed to get away for a while," she said. "It's nothing to worry about."

"Maya, you can't just disappear like this," Megan said, her voice taking on a desperate edge. "You're scaring me."

Maya hesitated. She knew it wasn't fair to keep secrets from her sister, especially after everything they'd been through together. But at the same time, she didn't want to put Megan in danger by telling her too much. "Look, Megan," she said. "I wish I could explain everything to you. But it's complicated. Just trust me when I say that I'm okay and I'll be back soon."

"Maya, why don't you tell me where you are and I'll come get you?" Megan said.

"Megan, I'm fine. Everything is fine. I'm just going to be a day or two, okay?"

There was a long pause on the other end of the line before Megan spoke again. "Okay," she said hesitantly. "But if you need anything, you know I'm here for you, right?"

Maya swallowed hard, feeling the weight of her sister's concern. "I know," she said. "Thanks, Megan. I appreciate it."

After they hung up, Maya sat on the edge of her bed, her mind racing. She knew that she couldn't keep avoiding the truth forever, but for now, she also knew that she had to. A life might depend on it.

Maya's mind kept racing as she went back to the files, trying to find a connection, an answer. She was still working on them when her head started to nod, and she finally gave in to the need to sleep.

*

The dream was far too familiar, one that had tormented Maya for months, if not longer. She was wandering a maze, looking for the Moonlight Killer, only these days, it wasn't a maze. It was the bunker. The same bunker from which Maya had rescued three of the women he'd taken.

Maya moved forward, flinching as the Moonlight Killer fired back at her, somewhere ahead. He wasn't wearing his mask in the dream, so that she could see Frank's face as he backed away through the twists and turns of the bunker, trying to kill Maya.

There were tripwires there that hadn't been there in real life, forcing her to tiptoe over them. Maya's heart was pounding, her palms sweaty as she navigated the maze. She knew she had to take out the Moonlight Killer before he could kill her. She spotted him ahead and took aim with her gun. But before she could shoot, he disappeared into the shadows.

Maya chased after him, her heart racing as she tried to keep up with his quick footsteps. It was like trying to catch a shadow in the darkness. But she didn't give up. She couldn't afford to.

Maya reached the central chamber, where the women had been held in cages. Only now, the only woman there in one of the cages was Megan, while in front of her...

Imogen's body hung there, alongside, improbably, Rose Kallen. Maya broke open the lock on her sister's cage, but she couldn't stop; she had to keep moving forward to catch the Moonlight Killer.

She moved through into the control room of the bunker, the room where she'd confronted the Moonlight Killer before, while he held Megan hostage.

It wasn't Megan now. It was Lucy, held tight back against him. His mask was back in place, too, so that Maya couldn't see his face.

Maya lifted her gun, ready to fire. Even as she did it, though, he lifted the trigger linked to the explosives in the bunker. He pressed the button.

There was no delay this time, no time to get clear. The bunker simply exploded around Maya, flames tearing around her, pain ripping through her...

Maya woke up in a cold sweat. It was still dark outside, but her phone told her that it was almost morning. Time to start the day, trying to find an answer in this case.

But what answers were there? She'd run down her first lead last night. What else was there?

Maya found herself thinking about the Moonlight Killer. Maybe it was just the dream, but she couldn't drag her thoughts from Frank Hanratty.

What had he said when she'd gone to see him? That there was more than one murder? Maybe the key to solving Rose's murder lay in finding who else had died.

CHAPTER SIXTEEN

A couple of hours later, and Maya was sitting in a local diner, still looking through the FBI's databases, hoping to find answers. She was on her fifth cup of coffee by now, maybe more, and a slice of cake stood untouched on the table in front of her.

It should have been simple to find cases similar to Rose Kallen's death if they were on the system. But as Maya scrolled through the lists of murders and unsolved cases, she found nothing local that matched the Moonlight Killer's signature. It was as if Rose Kallen's killer had appeared out of nowhere, leaving no trace behind him.

No, Maya wasn't going to believe that. There had to be answers. Frank Hanratty, the Moonlight Killer, had told her that not only was this not one of his kills, but that there was more than one murder, not just Rose Kallen's death.

Did Maya believe that? The man was a convicted serial killer, after all, one who always had his own plans. Maybe he was lying for his own ends. He wouldn't hesitate to do so if it got him closer to his goals.

Except that Maya believed him in this. Frank had always wanted Maya to investigate old murders ascribed to him, had been interested in clearing his names of the murders he didn't commit so that the dozen he claimed would stand out better. He also had no reason to lie about there being more than one murder. If he wanted Maya to find the truth here, lying would only distract her.

Was it possible that he was simply wrong? No, Maya didn't believe that either. Time and again, Frank had shown that his intelligence-gathering methods and deductive skills were more than up to the task of working out details that other investigators had missed. He'd always seemed to know, in at least general terms, who the killer was that Maya was hunting for.

Maya's phone beeped, a message from Marco. She ignored it, still focused on the database in front of her. She was a little worried about searching through the FBI databases like this in case any of her searches ended up being flagged. Maya had the authority to make these searches, but she didn't want to make it obvious that she was working on a case that the rest of the FBI didn't know about.

She checked FBI records, but also newspaper records. Maya hesitated briefly, then put in a call.

Samit was a tech who had worked on her short-lived task force dedicated to finding the man who had kidnapped her sister along with twelve other women. He was still working in the FBI, and Maya hoped that he was inclined to do her a favor.

"Hey, Samit. It's Maya. Listen, I need a favor," Maya said as soon as Samit picked up the phone.

"Hey, Maya. Sure, what do you need?" Samit replied.

"Is there any chance that you could get me access to police files for the town of Ellonsea, on the east coast? And possibly the surrounding area?"

"Okay, that's pretty specific. But I can do it. What's the context?" Samit questioned.

Maya hesitated, not sure if she should tell Samit about her unauthorized investigation. But she decided that she needed his help, and so she took a deep breath and said, "I'm investigating a murder case that I can't get any information on through official channels. I'm trying to find similar cases in the area to help me solve it."

There was a brief pause on the other end of the line before Samit said, "Okay, I'll see what I can do. Give me a few minutes."

"Thanks, Samit. You're a lifesaver," Maya said, relief flooding through her. She hung up and went back to her search, hoping that Samit would come through for her. If anyone could get her the information she needed without raising any red flags, it was Samit.

A few minutes later, a message pinged through to her phone, letting Maya know that she had the access she required. Maya leaned back in her chair, feeling a small sense of relief. At least she was getting somewhere.

She added the police files to her list of databases to search, looking through all the records she had for anything that might plausibly be a second murder by the same killer.

The first problem was that there were too many murders. Ellonsea might not be a major city, but it was still a large town, and every town had its problems. Particularly if she searched back for a few years. Her screen was filled with potential hits, but could she really go through them all, trying to find one with a potential connection? Just searching through every case could take her the rest of today. Maya needed a way to narrow things down.

Okay, so she needed to think about the kinds of connections that it would take for Maya to link a case to Rose Kallen's case. She guessed that it would be the murder of a woman, so Maya narrowed it down that way, but that didn't reduce the field of murders nearly enough to let her say that any one of them was potentially by the same killer. There were still also too many for her to simply go through them one by one, trying to look for something that fit.

There would be women who had been killed by their partners on this list, women who had gotten caught up in violent events or crime, women who had been the victims of home invasions or robberies.

Could Maya exclude solved murders? No, not when Rose Kallen's murder was supposedly solved, as the work of the Moonlight Killer. It was entirely possible that other murders by the same killer could be assumed to be someone else's work.

So then what? Could she limit this to kills made at night? That was easy enough to do, but it still didn't narrow things down enough, when more murders were committed under the cover of darkness than in the middle of the day.

Maya sat back in her chair, sipping her coffee as she thought. She needed a way to find a common thread among the potential cases that she could use to narrow them down further.

Maya tried narrowing it down to just murders committed under the full moon. She was good at finding the dates for the full moon and using them as a filter, when it had been a part of the Moonlight Killer's MO for years.

That narrowed things too much. All that was left was Rose's murder and a couple of killings that were quite obviously different. A woman gunned down as part of a robbery. One was stabbed in front of half a dozen witnesses by a jealous boyfriend. Neither was obviously connected to the death on the docks.

Maya cursed loud enough that it drew the attention of the server at the diner.

"Sorry," she said. "Can I get another coffee?"

She needed the steady stream of caffeine to help her think. Plus, it meant that she could keep working here in a booth of the diner, the other residents of Ellonsea chatting and moving around her. Maya carefully kept the screen angled so that they wouldn't see it. If someone did, her story about being a writer would probably be enough to explain the police files on her screen, but she didn't want to have the conversation.

She was missing something, but what? Her phone started to ring. Marco was calling, but Maya was so caught up in this now that she couldn't take the time to answer. In any case, she wasn't sure how to explain what she was doing to him. He would just worry and try to convince her to drop it. But Maya couldn't let this go. She had to find out if there was a connection, if there was another killer out there that the police had missed.

As she sipped her coffee, Maya's eyes scanned through the list of murders again, starting from the top. In frustration, she broadened her search to the entire Atlantic seaboard within a state or two either side of Ellonsea. Obviously, before she started to filter the search, there were way too many cases to look through. But she couldn't give up now.

She started to narrow things down, looking for the murder of a woman, at night. Maya didn't include the full moon this time, because there was always a chance that might have been a coincidence. Just because the Moonlight Killer always struck on the full moon, that didn't mean that someone whose work had been mistaken for his would necessarily stick to the same pattern.

Obviously, that still gave her too many results to look through, so many that Maya might still have been trying to wade after them long after the kidnapper's deadline passed if she tried.

Assume a killer who had killed more than once, the way the Moonlight Killer said. If they hadn't killed in an obvious group of victims, a spree, then it seemed likely that Maya was looking for the work of a serial killer. The Moonlight Killer had sent her after several such killers before.

One thing that tended to stay consistent for serial killers was their MO. Rose Kallen had been strangled with a rope. Checking for murders with that MO would reduce the number of potential cases a little, wouldn't it?

It reduced the numbers a lot, although there were still plenty of murders up and down the East Coast where women had been strangled with a rope at night.

Maya leaned back in her chair, staring at her screen as she rubbed her tired eyes. She had been at this for what seemed like forever now, and while she had narrowed down the list of potential cases significantly, she still didn't have a clear connection.

She took a deep breath, trying to clear her mind for a moment. Maybe she was overthinking this. Maybe the answer was right in front of her.

Maya started to read through the details of cases, moving quickly, hoping that something would stand out to her.

And then she saw it.

A case from three years ago, in Teaksville, a small town a state over from Ellonsea. A young woman, strangled with a rope at night. It had been a high-profile case at the time, details all over the local newspapers. Something caught her eye, a detail that she hadn't considered important.

The location of the murder. This woman had been killed on a local dock at night, just as Rose Kallen had.

That was enough to make Maya start looking at more of the details of the case. The victim's name was Emily Blackwell, and she was only 22 at the time of her murder. Maya quickly pulled up the news reports from that time, reading through them with a growing sense of unease. The similarities between Emily's murder and Rose's were striking. They had both been strangled with a rope, both at night and both on a dock.

The murder was still unsolved, but was this was interesting. Maybe it would even be enough to let Maya find answers on this case. She needed to make one phone call first.

Maya put a call through to the correctional facility holding Frank Hanratty.

"This is Agent Maya Gray, with the FBI," Maya said. "I'll give you my badge number. I need to speak to Michael Francis Hanratty. It's urgent."

Of course, it was never that simple, getting to talk to a convicted serial killer. The badge number helped, as did the fact that Maya had been to speak with Frank just the day before. Even so, she had to wait on the end of the line, holding for long minutes until, finally, Frank's voice came onto the call.

"Dear Maya, did you miss me?"

"I have a question for you."

"You want my help with your case?"

"I want you to confirm something for me. About the killer's other murders."

"I've told you that I won't give you the answers."

"I don't want you to give me anything, just confirm whether I've gotten this right. You do *want* the truth to come out, don't you?"

"Or for Lucy Barnet to pay with her life, and you to realize that you've gotten her killed," Frank replied.

Maya knew she had to play the card she had and hope. "Emily Blackwell."

There was a pause at the other end of the line. "Ah, it seems that you *are* getting somewhere."

That was enough for Maya. She hung up. She needed to get to Clarksville.

CHAPTER SEVENTEEN

Maya caught a flight over as close to Teaksville as she could get, then took an Uber the rest of the way into the town. The town was a small coastal place with a town center of restaurants, shops and other businesses. They lined the center of town, while homes and condos spread out to the north and south. The ocean had a salty scent that drifted up from the bay. The docks and boathouses smelled of fish, presumably a major industry in the town.

There was a sense of greater wealth there than there had been back in Ellonsea, though. The houses were old but carefully and expensively renovated. There were fishing boats down in the harbor, but also yachts, even a couple of larger private boats that could have been the property of millionaires.

Maya started to make her way through the town. She wasn't about to go down to the local police department after the reception she'd had in Ellonsea. Maya couldn't identify herself as an FBI agent without risking bringing in too much attention, but if she kept to her cover story as a writer, she couldn't push them to give her help or information.

Maya already had what had come up in her search, though. She had information on the case. She just needed to work out what it all meant and how it connected to Rose Kallen's murder.

Just. Maya almost laughed at that word. She'd hopped on a plane to a completely different town to investigate a murder in the hope that it would link back to a completely different murder and give her enough new information to let her get to the killer who had murdered both Rose and Emily. All because the Moonlight killer had confirmed for her that the same man had killed both.

Maya made her way towards the scene of Emily's murder. What she hadn't been able to get from police records, she'd been able to find in the local news, so she had an address for it, at least. Maya walked through the town, taking in the sights and sounds as she went. As she walked, she noticed a small bar on a side street. It was a little dive bar, with a neon sign that read "The Dockside". Maya passed by a few locals who gave her nods or smiled in greeting, and Maya returned the gestures politely.

When she reached the dock where Emily had been killed, Maya felt a chill run down her spine. She could almost see the scene play out in front of her. The water was still, glittering in the sunlight.

This harbor would have been beautiful, if Maya didn't know what had happened there. The air was crisp and clear, the sound of the lapping waves gentle. There were expensive restaurants around the harbor and plenty of places clearly aimed at tourists or boating enthusiasts.

The spot where Emily Blackwell had been murdered was near one such place: a boat rental business at the far end of the harbor. It seemed to be right around the spot where the expensive boats of the better off visitors gave way to less expensive craft that seemed to be working vehicles, fishing boats and more mundane things. They were a far cry from the sleek yachts at the other end of the harbor.

Maya had enough photographs from the time of the murder to be able to pin down the spot where Emily's body had been found . She approached the area and surveyed the surroundings. The dock had a small lighthouse on one end, and wooden pillars supported it. From her research, Maya knew that Emily had been found strangled by a rope, her body left against the wall of the business in front of her. . As she stood there, Maya could feel the tension rising within her. She couldn't believe that someone had been killed in such a peaceful and beautiful place. She wondered how the locals had responded to Emily's murder.

She walked over to the spot where Emily had been found and stood there for a moment, taking in the surroundings. The dock was narrow and rickety, with rusted metal supports and missing planks. The water was murky, and the boats around her creaked in the wind. It was no wonder that Emily's killer hadn't been caught. It was a secluded spot, away from the fancier parts of the harbor and all the cameras that would be covering that part.

Maya started to examine the area more closely, taking photos and making notes. She was looking for any clues that might lead her to the killer. After three years, though, there wasn't likely to be anything.

Maya considered the boat rental place. Was it possible that Emily had some connection to the business? The reports Maya had read had been patchy on that kind of detail, but Rose Kallen had been killed outside the spot where she worked. Was this about a killer targeting women who worked near docks, or had both victims just been in the wrong place at the wrong time?

Maya guessed that the people who worked in the boat rental business might know more. She guessed that they would have been the ones to find Emily, or at least that they might have heard some of the details at the time.

Maya went inside the rental business and was greeted by a young man behind the counter, maybe only twenty or so. The young man behind the counter was tall, and he had jet-black hair that fell across two startlingly green eyes. The tight leather of his jacket was the color of wet sand, and the buttons gleamed. He looked up at Maya and gave her a welcoming smile.

"Hi," he said. "I'm Ted. What can I do for you today? Are you here to rent a boat?"

Maya had to shake her head. "Sorry, no. I'm here about what happened to Emily Blackwell."

"That?" Ted said. "But that was years ago. Are you a cop?"

Maya shook her head. "I'm writing a book on strange murders. I heard about Emily's death, and I wanted to find out more."

"A writer?" Ted said. "That sounds like a cool job. Although I'm not sure how much I can tell you about what happened. I was just working here. It's not like they tell the boat rental guy all the details of everything."

"But my guess is that you heard rumors?" Maya said. "And if this happened so close to your place, you must have been interested."

"My uncle's place, technically," Ted said. "I just help him run it. It's pretty impressive, right?"

He gestured to the interior of the boat rental business. The front office in which he and Maya were standing was filled with nautical-themed oddities. The walls decorated with fishing lures. The desk had an old timey looking lamp of polished brass, with images of ships engraved on the glass. There were maps of far off places and pictures of what Maya assumed were satisfied clients out on boat trips. There was even a stuffed marlin on one wall. Even the counter behind which Ted was standing looked as though it had been made from the remains of an old boat.

Maya didn't have time for any of it right then. She was too busy staring at an object on the far wall. It was like a clock, wooden mounted, with the numbers one to five running up one side and down the other. It had the word "high" at the top and "low" at the bottom.

Maya stared at it because she'd seen something like it before at the shipping office where Rose Kallen had worked until the night of her death.

"What is that?" Maya asked, pointing.

Ted followed the line of her pointing finger and frowned. "That? That's just our tide clock. You know, to tell you when high and low tide are going to be?"

Maya didn't know, but the fact seemed to stick in her brain, refusing to let itself be dislodged. Was it just a coincidence that the places outside which both Rose and Emily had been killed had clocks like that? Probably, given the casualness with which Ted talked about it. Presumably, everyone along the harbor had something similar. They needed to know about the tides, needed to know when it would be easy to come and go.

That felt much more significant than the tide clock itself.

Both victims had died by the sea. Not just in coastal towns, but right by the water, within view of the vessels that came and went. Why was that when a killer could have chosen victims anywhere in the two towns?

Maya's mind raced with theories as she stared at the tide clock. Perhaps the killer was drawn to the water, or maybe they felt more comfortable committing their crimes there. No, it was more than that, it had to be.

"Did you know Emily Blackwell?" Maya asked, as much to give her time to think as anything.

Ted shook her head. "She was local, I think, but from what I heard, she was only down on the docks that night because she was heading out to dinner with a guy."

A guy the cops had presumably looked at. A guy who wasn't relevant, if the two deaths were linked. The answer wasn't in the specifics of Emily's life, or Rose's, but in the connections between their deaths.

"Are you okay?" Ted asked. "You seem to be staring at the tide clock."

"Sorry, just thinking," Maya said.

Specifically, thinking about the kinds of people who needed to know about the tides. The kinds of people who might murder two women in two different locations, but both of them right up against the ocean.

"He came in from the water!" Maya said aloud.

Ted frowned at her in confusion. "What?"

Maya shook her head. "Nothing. You've been very helpful. I need to go."

She hurried out of the boat rental office, trying to think. The more she thought, the more obvious her conclusion seemed. The killer was taking victims on the docks because they were victims of opportunity. They were there, in front of him, when he arrived in the towns. He killed victims in such distant towns because he was traveling between them. And he was traveling by water, because the docks were the first place he thought of to stalk his victims.

Maya was looking for someone connected to a boat that had been in both Ellonsea and Lakeville on the nights of the two victims' murders.

Now, she just had to find a way of working out which boats had been there.

CHAPTER EIGHTEEN

Maya found a spot not far from the water to think, settling on a bench that let her look out across the broad sweep of the harbor.

She watched the boats coming and going. The more she watched them, the more convinced she was about her conjecture that the killer was coming to the towns where he struck via the water.

It explained why he'd killed so close to the docks, why he'd killed in two coastal towns so far apart, maybe even said something about the manner of death. Was it possible that the rope he used was a ship's rope, and that was the reason that he strangled his victims like that? Maya fished her laptop out of her bag and called up pictures of the crime scene

photos. She zoomed in on the rope around Rose Kallen's neck. It looked thick and rough, definitely not the kind of rope you'd find in a hardware store.

Maya sighed, knowing that she needed more information to confirm her theory. She would need to find out which boats had been in both towns on the nights of the murders. She opened up a search engine and started trying to work out if there was a way to find out what she needed to know from that kind of publicly available source.

There wasn't, not that she could see. Which meant that she was going to have to do this another way. There would be a harbor clerk's office here somewhere. They would presumably have copies of shipping manifests for every vessel that came into the harbor, detailing the cargo, crew, and time of arrival.

Maya stood up from the bench and walked along the harbor, looking for the office. She looked up the location on her phone, trying to get her bearings. Maya kept going along the harbor side.

Would the killer's boat have registered? That was a worrying question. Officially, of course, it had to. But was there any chance that a boat could slip into the harbor unannounced while the killer committed murder and then slipped back out?

Maya wasn't sure. She suspected that even small harbors were watched more closely than that, and the location of the murders suggested that the killer was mooring his boat in the harbors, rather than making landfall in some secluded spot down the coast, the way a smuggler might. In any case, if there had been any sighting of some unauthorized boat slipping in like that, it would have raised suspicions that the local police would undoubtedly have acted on.

No, this was someone who was able to blend in, someone whose boat would be just another among the many that docked in the harbor. Someone who knew how to keep a low profile. They would have a legitimate reason to be in town. Probably, that reason would even be real, rather than something fabricated to get them there. Maya suspected that this killer was taking targets of opportunity rather than seeking out specific victims in specific places.

As she walked, Maya spotted the harbor clerk's office and made her way towards it. She hoped that the information she was looking for would be there, but she knew it wasn't going to be easy to get. The harbor clerk would probably be wary of sharing information with someone who wasn't from law enforcement, and Maya still didn't want to identify herself as FBI if she could avoid it.

But she was determined to try. She walked up to the door and took a deep breath before opening it. The scents of dust and paper hit her nose as she stepped inside, scents that she associated with officialdom everywhere. The front office was small, cramped, and cluttered with paperwork, although doors at the back of the room suggested other offices behind it. Behind the desk sat a middle-aged woman who looked up as Maya entered.

"Can I help you?" the woman asked, her voice clipped and professional.

Maya approached the desk, hoping that she could do this without breaking her cover.

"Yes, I'm looking for information on boats that were docked here on a specific date."

The man raised his eyebrows. "And what do you need that information for?"

Maya hesitated. Did she give this woman the truth, or did she continue with her story that she was a writer?

Maya took a deep breath, trying to keep her voice steady. "I'm a writer, doing research for a book. All about Emily Blackwell's murder. I need information on the boats that were docked here on the night of the murder. I want to make sure that I'm getting the details right."

The woman was already shaking her head

"I can't do that," she said. "I can't just hand out shipping information to anyone who asks."

"Can't I make a freedom of information request for the manifests?"

"You could," the woman said, "but that would have to be in writing, it would take several weeks to process, and those businesses that have put in an electronic shipping confidentiality request will be able to keep their manifests private."

There was no hint of give or helpfulness in her voice.

Maya tried to think of another way to get the information she needed. She couldn't afford to waste several weeks waiting for a written request to be processed. She needed to find a way to get the information now.

The worst part was that she had one. It was just one that she hadn't wanted to use.

Maya flashed her badge. Not for long, certainly not long enough for the woman to get her name, but long enough for her to see it.

"Look," she said, leaning in towards the woman. "I understand that you can't just hand out confidential information like that. But this is important. Lives are at stake. I need to know who was here on that night so that I can help catch the person responsible for these murders."

Maya saw the clerk's eyes widen slightly. "I... I'm still not sure what I can do. I would have to make a call to check."

"I understand," Maya said, although it was frustrating. She needed that information.

The woman headed off into a back room to make the call, leaving her station behind her computer. It occurred to Maya as the woman left that the call probably wouldn't go her way. The clerk would want a warrant, or at least an official written request that might still take days to deal with. Maya didn't have days.

She had to act now. If she didn't, then Lucy Barnet would die. Possibly other women would too, if this really was a serial killer.

Maya hurried behind the desk to the still unlocked computer, trying not to think about just how illegal this was. With lives at stake, she wasn't sure that she had another choice.

Maya worked quickly, looking for the shipping manifests from the date of Emily Blackwell's murder. She found them, along with the manifests for a day either side, just to be safe.

Maya quickly downloaded them onto a flash drive, looking over her shoulder for any sign of the clerk. Maya pocketed the drive, closed the files on the computer, and quickly hurried back around to the correct side of the desk.

She made it just in time to see the clerk returning to the front office. Maya took a deep breath, trying to calm her racing heart as she waited for the clerk to speak.

"I'm sorry," the woman said, looking apologetic. "I can't just give out confidential information like that. You would need to put in an official request. However, I can tell you that there were several boats docked here on the night of Emily Blackwell's murder."

Maya nodded, trying to keep her expression neutral, maybe trying to feign a hint of disappointment. "Thank you for your help."

She turned to head out of the office, her mind racing with the possibilities that the manifests might hold. She needed to find a quiet place to review them, to see what was there.

Maya stepped out of the office and into the cool afternoon air. She made her way down the street and into a nearby coffee shop. The place was empty, and the barista seemed too lost in thought to even notice Maya as she walked in. Maya ordered a black coffee and sat down at a table in the corner.

She pulled out the flash drive and plugged it into her laptop. She opened the manifests, scanning through the list of ships and their cargo. Most of it was unremarkable, just shipments of goods from one port to another and lists of crew. But one of these ships, she guessed, had been carrying a killer.

The trouble was working out which one. It seemed clear now that there wasn't going to be anything within the manifests that would let her single out one ship over another. There wasn't anything about the time of arrival or the contents of the cargo that would point to one boat holding a serial killer when another did not. That was a part of how the killer stayed hidden, making everything he did seem ordinary.

The only way to narrow down the field of boats that could have carried the killer was to find the equivalent manifests from Ellonsea.

Maya already knew that she couldn't go back there to ask for them. It would take too much time, and she'd already seen the kind of response that she was likely to get. No, she would have to find some other way to get her hands on those manifests.

Maya took a sip of her coffee, thinking hard. She needed to find someone who could help her, someone who wouldn't ask too many questions. On another occasion, Maya might have asked Marco, but then she would have to explain what she was doing, and why. In any case, gathering information like that wasn't his forte. He was better at being on the ground, investigating.

Maya missed him, but it wasn't Marco she called.

"Agent Gray?" Samit said as he picked up. "Calling again so soon?"

Maya took a deep breath before answering, knowing that there would be no turning back once she said this. "I need another favor," she said, her voice low and urgent.

"What kind of favor?" Samit asked. The tech sounded a little worried. "Getting you access to more police files?"

"I need you to get me access to the shipping manifests from a town called Ellonsea for the 20th August. Maybe a day either side, too."

"You could just put in a request for them," Samit said. "Maybe get a warrant for them if the shipping office isn't cooperating. Are you *in* Ellonsea?"

"Not right now," Maya replied. "And I can't do it that way. It would take too long."

"Too long for what?" Samit was silent for a moment. "Maya, what's going on? Why do you need those manifests?"

"I think I'm onto something big here, Samit," Maya replied. "It's probably safer for you if I don't give you the details, but... lives are at stake. If I don't get this information, someone could die."

Samit hesitated. "I'll need more than that. What you're asking... I would need to hack their systems."

Maya knew that, but she wasn't sure how much she could risk telling him. On the other hand, he'd worked with Maya on her task force. He knew the kinds of situations she could be faced with.

"It's happening again, Samit," Maya said. "One of the women from the bunker, Lucy Barnet, went missing. Then I got a postcard."

"That's..." There was a long, horrified pause on the other end of the line. "Does Marco know?"

"Not yet. I can't get the rest of the FBI involved. I barely dare ask you for this. Samit, can you do this for me?"

Another pause. Maya imagined Samit considering it.

"Let me think about it," he said. He hung up.

Maya wasn't sure then if she'd done the right thing or not. She could see why Samit might not want to help her. He could get into trouble for doing it when this was something unofficial, might even lose his job.

Maya just had to hope that he would come through for her.

CHAPTER NINETEEN

Maya wanted to find a way to make progress while she waited and hoped that Samit would get back to her with the information she needed. Ordinarily, she would have found someone else to question, searched for a witness who might have seen something.

Now, instead of that, she found her attention caught by the idea of tide clocks. Something at the back of her mind insisted that they were important, even though they couldn't be. The tide clocks had been inside the buildings the two victims had been killed outside. The killer wouldn't even have known that they were there.

Even so, she took a moment or two to do research on them. The basics were easy enough to find: tide clocks were used to track the tide levels in coastal areas, and they were often found on docks and piers. She looked at their history, and found that early examples dated back as far as 17th century England, when tidal information started to be included in other clocks. The first modern examples appeared in 1890, based on a dial tracking a period of 12 hours, 25 minutes and 14 seconds, the average tidal period. Maya looked at fine examples, and at cheaper modern ones.

She realized, though, that the point wasn't the tide clocks. At least she assumed it wasn't, because there was no way that the killer could have seen the tide clocks in the places where the victims had been killed. The tides themselves, though? Could they matter? She started to go back through the files she had access to for the murders, trying to find some reference to the likely times of death for both Rose Kallen and Emily Blackwell.

Maya found those eventually. Then looked online for a resource that would give her the tide levels in different places at different times.

As she compared the tides with the times of death, a pattern started to emerge. Both women had been killed at high tide, right when the water level was at its highest point. Both Rose and Emily had been killed during high tide, with the water level almost reaching the docks where they were found. It couldn't be a coincidence.

Maya's mind raced as she tried to make sense of it. Was it a way for the killer to hide evidence? Or was it symbolic in some way? She needed more information to be sure.

Perhaps the high tide angle was why Rose Kallen had been killed on the full moon, when it would contribute to a higher tide than usual. A coincidence that had pointed people wrongly at the Moonlight Killer.

Maya was still contemplating the significance of that when her phone rang. Maya answered it without thinking, breathing a sigh of relief.

"Samit, talk to me."

"You were expecting a call from Samit?" Marco said. Maya cursed to herself, even though it was good to hear his voice. She'd been trying to avoid a difficult conversation with him since the start of this. She still couldn't tell him everything, because it would put him in too difficult a position. It might endanger everything he'd built by becoming an FBI agent if Maya's superiors suspected that he'd helped her in this.

"Yes," Maya said. "It's nothing important."

"Nothing important, but you needed to call Samit?"

"I just... wanted to see what he remembered about some of the things that happened back when he was on the task force. A different view on it."

Maya hated lying to Marco like that, but it was the only way to keep him safely out of this.

Safe for whom? Maya was telling herself that it meant that Marco wouldn't have any fallout from their superiors over this, but it also meant that he couldn't try to talk her out of this case, and couldn't *tell* their superiors anything that might bring the full weight of the FBI in on the case. That would definitely break the kidnapper's rules, definitely get Lucy killed. Maya couldn't risk that. She'd had to tell Samit, but even that had been a risk. Marco... as much as she loved him, he didn't need to know.

"So you're working on your book somewhere?" Marco said. "Only your messages were about a family emergency, and Megan didn't know anything about a family emergency. Or about a Cousin Barney. What's going on, Maya?"

Maya could hear the worry there in his voice.

She felt a pang of guilt for lying to him, but she knew that she couldn't tell him the truth. Not yet. Not until she had solid evidence and a way to bring down the killer without endangering Lucy's life.

"Yes, I’m working on the book," Maya said, hoping that it sounded convincing. "Just trying to get some research done."

There was a moment of silence on the other end of the line. Maya could hear Marco breathing, could almost feel his presence even though he was miles away.

"So why say that it was a family emergency?" Marco asked. “Why invent a fake cousin?”

That was the problem with having an FBI agent and former cop for a fiance. He wasn't going to let anything go that didn't fit.

"That was..." Maya improvised furiously, and realized that a part of the truth was her friend here. "Look, I know that was stupid. I didn't want to worry you or Megan. I knew that my book was a problem for Megan, and I thought it would worry you if I told you that I'd gone off to work on it."

"So you're... what? Off on some kind of writer's retreat?" Marco asked.

"Doing some research and writing as I go," Maya replied.

"What kind of research?"

"Marco, you don't need to worry about me," Maya said. She hoped that it was true. "Everything here is okay, and I'll be home soon."

"Maya, you know I can tell when you’re lying to me." Marco said, sounding suddenly suspicious. “Are you sure everything is okay?”

Maya sighed. She wished she could tell Marco everything, but she couldn't risk it. Not yet.

"I'm sure," Maya said firmly. "I'll see you soon, okay?"

"Okay," Marco said, and she could hear the reluctance in his voice. "Whatever this is, be careful, Maya. I don't want anything to happen to you."

"I will," Maya promised, and then hung up.

She leaned back in her chair and closed her eyes, letting out a deep breath. She couldn't afford to let her emotions get the best of her right now. She needed to focus on finding a killer.

Her phone rang again and this time, Maya checked it before answering. It was Samit.

"Hi Samit," Maya said.

"Hey Maya," Samit said. "I did some digging like you asked. I found the data you wanted, and I've sent it to you."

"Thanks," Maya said.

"Are you sure it's a good idea to do this alone?" Samit asked.

"I don't have another choice, not in this. Thank you, Samit."

Maya hung up, going back to her laptop and pulling up the data Samit had sent. He'd managed to get the Ellonsea shipping manifests for the dates around Rose Kallen's murder. Maya wasn't sure what he would have had to do to get them, but she guessed that it had involved hacking his way into the systems of the shipping office. There had certainly been no time to put in a formal request.

Now, Maya had the shipping manifests from Ellonsea around the time of Rose Kallen's death. She had the equivalent manifests for Teaksville on the night of Emily Blackwell's murder.

Maya started to compare the two manifests, looking for any similarities, any ships that had been in both places on the days of the murders.

As she worked, Maya's mind wandered back to Lucy. She couldn't imagine what it must be like for her, trapped in the hands of her kidnapper. Maya felt a surge of anger towards the man who had taken her, but she quickly pushed it aside. Anger wasn't going to help her find Lucy.

She couldn't find any ships on both lists at first, but maybe that was a good thing. The last thing Maya wanted was for there to be too many ships that might have carried the killer. As she continued to analyze the data, something caught her eye.

There was one ship that appeared in both manifests on the nights of the murders. It was a ship named "Moonlight Serenade." Maya's heart raced as she realized the potential significance of that. She kept going through the manifests, though, wanting to make sure that there weren't any other ships that had been in both towns on the days of the murders.

Maya checked every record, every ship name. To her relief, no other ships appeared on both lists. There was only the Moonlight Serenade.

If Maya's theory was right, *that* was the ship that had brought the killer to the places where he'd killed his victims. She quickly did a search for the ship, trying to find any additional information about it. She discovered that it was owned by a company called Seabreeze Industries and that it regularly traveled up and down the Atlantic seaboard, carrying cargo between stops, taking passengers, and occasionally getting rented out for a day or two.

Maya checked the ship's manifests, wanting to see its cargo and crew. The cargo varied between the two lists; it seemed that the Moonlight Serenade carried whatever its owners could get a contract to transport. There even appeared to have been a passenger at Ellonsea, although they weren't on the manifest for Teaksville.

The crew was the same each time. Maya had half hoped that the ship would only have one crew member common to both locations, but instead, the same half-dozen names appeared on both lists.

Six names, and one of them was the killer. Maya's mind was racing as she tried to piece together the identity of the killer. She couldn't believe that she had finally found a lead. The Moonlight Serenade was her ticket to finding the killer responsible for the deaths of Rose Kallen and Emily Blackwell.

She quickly searched for information on the crew members. There were no photos available, but she managed to find out their names and addresses. Most of them were based in a small town in Maine, near where the Moonlight Serenade was registered.

Maya realized that she wasn't going to find the killer through that kind of research. There was no way of picking one man out of the six. There was nothing that obviously stood out as a red flag.

Which meant that the ship was what mattered. Maya needed to find that ship, because the killer would be on it. Maybe if he arrived somewhere new at a high tide, he might even kill again.

Boats had GPS trackers on them, didn't they? Particularly with commercial vessels, their locations were easy to track, both to reduce the risks of collisions at sea and to allow their parent companies to watch their progress.

Maya went searching for a site that tracked ocean traffic and looked for the Moonlight Serenade. The manifests she possessed had the serial numbers she needed to be able to find it, typing those numbers into the site and waiting for the results.

Those results showed its current location, making its way along the coast. It also showed the destination it was heading for: a town named Harbor Bay, which was a small coastal town in Virginia..

Maya's heart raced as she realized she could intercept the ship there. She quickly looked up the best way to get to Harbor Bay and realized that it didn't have an airport near it, but it *was* just within driving distance.

Maya packed away her things in her bag, paid her check at the cafe she was sitting in, then caught the proprietor's attention for a moment.

"Hey, is there anywhere around here I can rent a car? I need to get up the coast in a hurry."

CHAPTER TWENTY

Lucy sat in her cage, waiting for the moment when her captor would either let her go or kill her.

By now, the terror of it all had turned from something sharp edged and panic inducing to something more like a dull ache of fear, refusing to go away. Yet she wasn't about to give up. Lucy was constantly looking around for a way to escape.

She tried to find a way out of the cage, but it was hopeless. The metal was too thick, and the lock too sturdy. It seemed as though the only way out was through her captor's mercy.

But there was no mercy from him. He appeared every so often, bringing her food and water, lecturing her about the importance of Maya Gray solving the murder of Rose Kallen.

Lucy couldn't understand why he was so invested in this case. Why did he care whether or not Maya solved it? Maybe, if she couldn't escape, she could at least find out that. She could have information to give Maya when she solved the case and got Lucy out of there.

Lucy trusted that she would, just as she had with the others. She would find out why this man was doing this, why he cared about the Moonlight Killer's cases. She would take that back to Maya.

But then, why had the Moonlight Killer cared? Why had he wanted her to clear his name of murders that weren't his, when he had committed so many others?

The man who'd kidnapped her had left her alone for now, still contained in her cage, when Francis Hanratty had frequently allowed Lucy and his other "bunnies" to walk his bunker complex freely.

It was strange, being alone here like this. Lucy was used to solitude, living in a cabin in the forest as she did. But this was a different kind of solitude, one where she was completely cut off from the outside world, with no way of knowing what was happening beyond the walls of her cage.

With the Moonlight Killer, there had been other women there in his bunker, held in cages alongside her. Now, Lucy could see other empty cages, but there was no sign of any other women.

It was just her there, waiting to see what would happen to her. Her mind kept wandering back to her captivity, to the man who held her captive. Who was he? Why was he doing this? Was it really possible that he was copying the work of a serial killer?

Lucy jumped as she heard footsteps approaching. Her captor was back. She looked up to see him approaching, dressed differently to how he had been when he first brought her there. Now he was in a suit and tie, with glasses perched on his nose. He set down the tray of food and water on the ground outside her cage before stepping back and watching her.

Lucy grabbed for the contents of the tray. Energy bars, a soft drink, nothing home prepared.

"I hope you're feeling well today, Lucy," he said, his tone almost conversational. It was bizarre the way he could act so calmly while keeping her locked up like an animal.

Lucy didn't respond, simply watching him warily. She didn't know what to say to him, how to even begin to understand what he wanted from her.

Lucy's abductor was oddly ordinary, not at all like the Moonlight Killer had been. Francis Hanratty had been terrifying and mercurial, equally likely to sing to the women he held hostage or lash out at them, to treat them with exaggerated care or hurt them. This man just seemed like he was trying to do this in as professional a fashion as he could.

"Why are you doing this?" Lucy asked.

"You know why I've kidnapped you," he replied. "Maya Gray has a task to perform, a murder to solve. If she does that, you go free."

"Yes, but *why*?" Lucy asked. "The Moonlight Killer... well, at least they were crimes he'd supposedly committed that Maya had to solve. Why do you care if Maya solves some old murder?"

"Maybe I can just see the purity of the Moonlight Killer's work," her captor suggested. "Maybe I understand more than you do."

Lucy scoffed. "The purity of a serial killer's work? That's twisted."

Her captor shrugged. "Perhaps. But that's not for you to decide, is it?"

Lucy glared at him, her fingers tightening around the energy bar. "What is it you see that makes his work pure?"

Her captor just smiled. "I suspect you wouldn't understand. He took people about to change, about to twist the world out of the order that had been set, and he took that change from them. He refocused it, altered the whole course of the world. There's power in that."

It sounded like a truly mad reason. It was obvious that this man wasn't just some hired help, he really believed in the Moonlight Killer's twisted vision of the world.

Lucy sighed. "What happens if Maya doesn't solve the murder in time?"

"You know the answer to that," her captor said.

"And you could do that? You could just kill me?" Lucy asked. She wanted to see if this man was another psychopath like Hanratty, or just some deluded follower who might still be reasoned with.

Her captor smiled. "Another day or so, and you'll get to find out. Agent Gray is running out of time, and so are you."

CHAPTER TWENTY ONE

Maya was driving a lot faster than she should have been, especially given that she was in a rented car. It didn't have lights or a siren, didn't have anything that would keep the cops from pulling her over or keep other traffic out of her way as she sped along the road. She tried to console herself with the fact that she'd signed the insurance waiver and kept her foot on the gas.

It helped that the roads she was taking didn't have a lot of traffic, which meant that Maya was making good time. Even so, she didn't dare to slow down for a moment. If the Moonlight Serenade reached its next destination before Maya got there, she had no guarantee that she would be able to find the killer. If he heard that someone was looking for him while he was off the ship, maybe he would run. If he did, Maya might not be able to find him again before the kidnapper's deadline.

Maya's mind was racing as she drove towards Harbor Bay. She kept going over what she knew about the killer, trying to piece together any clues that might lead her to him. But everything she had didn't add up to much.

Maya had to get to Harbor Bay before the Moonlight Serenade. She knew that the man who killed Rose Kallen and Emily Blackwell was on that ship. She was determined to get to him before he could escape.

A truck was ahead. Maya pulled around it, taking a corner while barely slowing down. As Maya's car screeched around the corner, she saw the sign for Harbor Bay up ahead. Relief flooded through her. She was almost there. She pressed down harder on the gas pedal, her eyes scanning the road for any dangers.

Harbor Bay came into view around the bend. It seemed to be the type of town that was full of life. Two large hills rose up from behind the town, like the shoulders of a sleeping giant. A mansion or two could be seen through the clear night air, set on top of the first hill -- one whole side of the house made of glass, looking out over the ocean. To Maya, it looked like a place she could never imagine living. It was too quiet compared to DC.

Although if she was right, it would soon play host to a killer. Maya kept driving towards it, heading into the town. People were walking on the streets, rain coming down steadily, their umbrellas bouncing in the wind.

The houses were small and stood in neat rows, with smaller stores and bars set between them. Maya made her way to the docks, hoping that she would be there before the Moonlight Serenade managed to dock.

Maya checked the website that she'd been using to track it. It seemed that the ship was getting close to port, but wasn't there yet.

Maya looked out and spotted a ship in the distance, its lights cutting through the rain. It was a small cargo ship, slightly dirty and rusty, the kind of vessel that had obviously seen hard work. She knew that she had to hurry. She parked the car and jumped out, running towards the docks. She could hear the sound of the ship's engines, growing louder as it approached.

She reached the dock just as the Moonlight Serenade was pulling in, moving towards a berth among the other boats gathered in the harbor. Maya knew that she had to get to the ship before it docked, or the killer might slip away. She parked the car, grabbed her gun from the glove compartment, and ran towards the dock.

Maya waited on the edge of the dock, watching as the Moonlight Serenade approached. Its crew worked on the deck, getting ready to moor it. Maya watched them as they worked, as if that might somehow let her pick out the killer. But it wasn't possible to pick out killers like that just by looking at them. It didn't work like that.

Waiting was the hardest part, there on the dock. Maya wasn't sure what she looked like standing there, waiting, the way some sweetheart might have waited for one of the sailors, or someone looking to book passage to the next port might have waited to speak to the captain.

The ship slowly pulled up to the dock. Maya watched as the crew members began to secure the ship with ropes, tying it tightly so it wouldn't drift away. She knew she had to move quickly.

Maya's heart was pounding as she approached the ship, her gun firmly in her hand. She could feel the rain soaking through her clothing, but she didn't care. All she could think about was getting to the killer before he made his escape.

She waited until the ship put down a gangway, ready for its crew to start unloading some of the cargo on it.

The moment it was down, Maya rushed up it, badge and gun at the ready. This was no moment in which to keep up her cover as a writer.

One of the crew moved to intercept her. He was a stocky man with a thick mustache and curly hair. He was dressed in baggy, dark clothing.

"Hey, where do you think you're going?"

The rain was falling on Maya's face. She didn't have any time for this. The man was in Maya's way, so she shoved him aside. The man's hand grabbed Maya's arm and she turned to him, lifting her badge.

"FBI, step aside." The crewman hesitated for a moment before moving out of her way.

The other crew members looked at her with surprise and apprehension, but Maya didn't have time to worry about their reactions. It was more important to find out which of them was a killer, which of them had slain both Rose Kallen and Emily Blackwell.

Maya stepped onto the ship's deck, scanning her surroundings. The smell of the ocean mixed with the scent of diesel fuel, overwhelming her senses.

An older man moved towards Maya. He wore the same uniform as the rest of the crew, but he didn't look like he fit in, more like he was the pilot or captain of the vessel. He had a thick beard and dark, bushy eyebrows.

"Who are you, and what are you doing on my boat?"

Maya took a deep breath and tried to stay calm. She could feel the weight of the man's gaze on her, and she knew she had to tread carefully.

"I'm Agent Maya Gray with the FBI. And you are?"

"I'm Captain Baird."

"Well, Captain, I need to ask you a few questions about your recent voyage. I believe... I believe that you may have a killer on your boat."

The man's expression grew even more skeptical. "I don't know what you're talking about. We're just a cargo vessel. Are you even really with the FBI? Some random woman jumps onto my boat, and I'm meant to take her at her word? Guys, get on with unloading."

Maya stepped between the men and the gangway. She still had her gun in her hand, although she was careful not to raise it. She raised her badge instead as a reminder of just who she was.

"No one is leaving this ship until I get answers," Maya called out. "I will arrest anyone who tries."

As the crew members exchanged uneasy glances, Maya scanned the deck, trying to pick out any signs of guilt or nervousness.

"You can't do this," Captain Baird said. "What are you going to arrest them for? You have no proof. Now, either put down that gun or leave my ship."

Maya didn't budge, keeping her eyes trained on the crew. She was sure the killer was here. She just had to find out who it was and gather the evidence.

"Proof?" Maya said. "Two women died on the nights your ship docked at their towns. The Moonlight Serenade is the *only* vessel that was present in both locations."

"This is about Rose Kallen and Emily Blackwell?" Captain Baird asked.

"You know about them?" Maya countered.

"Of course I know about them," the captain snapped back. "You think we're not going to hear about two murders in the places we visited? It doesn't mean that any of my crew had anything to do with it?"

Maya nodded, understanding the captain's position. "I know that it's a big accusation, but I have reason to believe that the killer is onboard your ship."

"And what reason is that?" Captain Baird asked, his voice laced with disbelief. "As far as I can tell, all you have is conjecture based on the coincidence of my ship being in both towns."

"The *only* ship docked in both places," Maya repeated, because that was the crucial point. This ship represented the only link between the two towns on the nights of the victims' deaths. "So now, I need to know about the movements of your crew when you docked in Ellonsea and Teaksville."

Captain Baird sighed and rubbed his forehead, as if he was considering Maya's request. "Fine. But you have to understand that my crew is innocent. They have nothing to do with this."

"And how can you be so sure?" Maya demanded. "I assume you didn't follow them all over the two towns when you came into port."

"No," Captain Baird said, "but I *did* pay for my guys to have a nice hotel for the night in Teaksville. We were all there, all night, or in the bar next door. I'll give you the details. If you're really FBI, that should be easy to check."

Maya felt a sudden sinking feeling, because it *would* be easy to check.

"How about it, lads?" Captain Baird said. "Was everyone with me at the hotel in Clarksville?"

A chorus of assent came from the crew.

"And did anyone see anyone sneak off to... what? Go kill someone?"

That got laughs from his crew, but they also shook their heads. Assuming that they weren't covering for one of their number, that meant that none of them could be the killer. Even if they were, it would be easy to check with the hotel. The hotel would have cameras. It would be easy to tell if one of them had slipped away.

No, they all had an alibi, one that would be easy to check, which meant... Maya was looking in the wrong place.

"I think it's time you got off my boat," Captain Baird said. "Coming here, harassing my crew. I'm going to complain to your bosses about this! Now off, off my boat!"

Maya gave in, knowing that she had hit a dead end. She holstered her gun and stepped back onto the dock. As she walked away, she couldn't help but feel a sense of frustration and disappointment wash over her. She had been so certain that the killer was on that ship, but now she was back to square one.

She couldn't see how. This boat was the obvious lead, the only vessel that had been in both places. Maya had needed to follow up on it, but now... she'd wasted precious time chasing a dead end, and worse, it seemed that her superiors were going to hear about it.

CHAPTER TWENTY TWO

The first call came while Maya was still sitting on the docks, trying to wrap her mind around where she'd gone wrong. The moment she saw Deputy Director Swift's name, she knew that this was going to be bad, but she still picked up. That wasn't the kind of call she could ignore and still keep her job.

"Agent Gray," Swift said, her voice clipped and professional, but still loaded with anger. "Do you want to tell me exactly what's going on?"

"About?" Maya said. She tried to work out the best way to manage the situation as she said it.

"The FBI just received a complaint from Captain Baird of some ship called the Moonlight Serenade. He claims that you harassed his crew and accused them of murder without any evidence." Swift paused. "Which fits with your general style, and wouldn't normally cross my desk. I'm not meant to be your boss."

"So why are you the one calling me?" Maya asked. She gritted her teeth, trying to keep her emotions in check.

"You know exactly why," Agent Swift snapped back. "The murder of Rose Kallen was mentioned. A murder for which the Moonlight Killer was convicted. As the head of the task force assigned to catching him, I was informed as a courtesy."

"A courtesy?" Maya said, not quite believing it.

"Actually, Agent Gray, people assumed that I had sent you out on this. Because you were technically working for my team when you caught Hanratty, they assumed that you wouldn't conduct some fresh investigation into one of his kills without so much as *informing* me."

Now, the anger in her voice was palpable.

Maya sighed. "I was just following up on a lead."

"A lead in a case that has already been closed," Swift retorted, without any give in her voice. "I told you before not to go trying to reopening those cases when it risks Hanratty's conviction."

"I'm certain that he didn't kill Rose Kallen," Maya said. "There's another serial killer out there, Swift, one who has killed at least two women, probably more. I'm making progress in the case."

"Forgive me if I don't trust your judgement, Gray," Swift said. "Not after you've run off to pursue your own investigation, wrongly accused someone, and gotten complaints sent through to my desk."

"You aren't my boss anymore, Swift," Maya pointed out.

"Which is just as well, because if I were, I'd probably fire you. As it is... if this causes any trouble for me, you're going to wish you'd never joined the Bureau."

It wasn't an empty threat. Swift was good at playing the internal politics of the FBI. She'd risen to a prominent position as a deputy director on the back of the Moonlight Killer case. Maya doubted that she would have any trouble getting Maya suspended or even fired if she wanted.

"You need to come back to DC," Swift said. "We'll sort this out here."

"You know I won't be able to get there today," Maya replied.

"Then tomorrow. But you *will* be here, and if you're lucky, I'll have calmed down enough by then that I don't push to have you fired for pursuing this investigation."

Swift hung up. Her anger still seemed to hang in the air afterwards like a cloud. Maya sat there for a moment, staring blankly at her phone. She knew Swift had the power to ruin her career, and she couldn't afford to lose her job. After everything that had happened, she wouldn't be surprised if Swift *did* push for some kind of reprimand.

Maya sat there, feeling a mix of anger and frustration that threatened to bubble over. She knew that she was onto something with the Moonlight Killer case, and her gut instinct told her that there was another killer out there. She couldn't just sit back and watch as innocent people were killed, especially when Lucy Barnet's life was on the line.

The threat to Lucy meant that she couldn't give up on this. She could agree to meet Swift some time tomorrow, because at midnight tonight, Maya would either have found the answer, or Lucy would die.

Maya couldn't let that happen, but she also couldn't see what she was meant to do to stop it. It was already afternoon, and Maya had been left without any leads.

She headed along the dock, trying to find somewhere to sit and think. She probably needed to find something to eat after the drive up the coast. It felt like she'd conducted half of this investigation out of coffee shops and diners.

Maya walked along the dock, searching for a place to eat. She breathed in the salty air, letting the sound of the waves soothe her frayed nerves. She needed to think. She needed to come up with something, anything, to save Lucy.

As she walked, she saw a small, dingy-looking bar nestled in amongst the fishing boats. The sign hanging outside read "The Salty Dog". It wasn't the kind of place she would normally choose, but it would do for now.

Maya pushed open the door and stepped inside. The interior was dimly lit, with a mixture of locals and tourists huddled around the bar. The smell of stale beer and fried food hit her as she made her way to an empty table in the corner. She resisted the urge to order a beer while she was working a case, reminding herself that she *was* still working it, and ordered coffee and snacks instead. She sat there, staring at her laptop, trying to work out where she'd gone wrong.

Her phone rang again, and Maya felt so empty, so wrung out after her conversation with Swift that she almost didn't answer it.

It was Marco, and that made it even harder to answer, but Maya knew that she didn't have a choice.

"Hey, Marco," Maya said, trying to keep her voice steady.

"Maya, I just got a call from Agent... sorry, Deputy Director Swift," Marco said, his voice filled with concern. "Maya, you told me that you were doing research for your book. You lied to me."

Maya's heart sank as she heard Marco's words. She had known that lying to him was wrong, but she couldn't tell him the truth about her investigation. Not when she knew that he could end up in trouble for getting involved. Not when he might try to stop her, too.

"I'm sorry, Marco," Maya said. "I didn't want to lie to you, but I couldn't tell you the truth. And I am... I'm looking into Rose Kallen's murder. And the murder of a woman called-"

"Emily Blackwell, I heard from Swift," Marco said. "So you've gone off, alone, to look into a cold case, and you've found another victim?"

"I know how that sounds," Maya said.

There was a pause at the other end of the line. "I don't think you do, Maya. Because it sounds... pretty obsessed, frankly."

"Obsessed?" That was a difficult word to hear. Maya felt a flash of anger. She wasn't obsessed, she was diligent. She was doing what needed to be done to solve these murders, even if it meant going against the wishes of her superiors. But she knew that getting into an argument with Marco wasn't going to help her case.

"I'm sorry you feel that way," Maya said, trying to keep her voice level. "But I believe that I'm onto something. There's another killer out there, and he's still active. I can't just sit back and watch as innocent people are killed."

"I understand that, Maya," Marco said, his voice softening. "But you must see what this is doing to you. You've already upset your sister Megan with this. You've created trouble for yourself at work. You've lied to me. I'm your fiance, and I was your partner. With all of that, don't you think this is going too far?"

"Look, Marco, I know how this sounds," Maya said, trying to keep her voice calm. "But I'm not giving up on this. And I'm the head of a field office. I get to assign cases. I can assign myself to this."

"To what, Maya?"

"There's another killer out there, I can feel it. And I need to find them before they hurt anyone else."

"I understand that, Maya," Marco said, his voice softening. "But I really think that you should come back to DC."

"I'm not sure I can do that," Maya said. "Not yet."

Perhaps if he hadn't accused her of being obsessed, Maya might have explained the truth of what was going on to Marco. Perhaps if there hadn't been the risk of him trying to find the kidnapper, putting Lucy in greater peril, she might have told him about the postcard, about the danger to Lucy, about all of it.

But now, all she felt was a pang of hurt. "I need to go," she said, her voice tight.

"Maya, wait," Marco said. "I can't come down there because of my investigation. But Megan has already told me that she's planning to come down to bring you back. She's already on her way."

"You talked to Megan before me on this?" Maya said.

"I wanted to talk to someone else who knew you, who could guess what was going on with you. Your sister seemed like the safest bet and also the best way to get you home."

"I'm not coming home yet," Maya said. "Not until this is done."

"This is done, Maya," Marco insisted.

Maya couldn't get into that argument with him.

"I'll talk to you later." She hung up before he could respond, feeling the tears prickling at the corners of her eyes.

Maya took a deep breath and looked around the bar, trying to push her emotions aside.

It didn't work. She had rarely felt as alone as she did right then. Somehow, this case had managed to alienate all the people she loved. It had managed to cut her off from her job and from all the support she might have gotten from the FBI.

She had been lying to him, and she had been neglecting her other responsibilities. But she couldn't just give up on this case. She had to find the killer before he struck again.

The trouble was, she didn't know how. She had to find another lead, but she wasn't sure what other leads there were, and she didn't have a lot of time to find them.

At midnight tonight, Lucy Barnet would die.

CHAPTER TWENTY THREE

Maya stared at her computer, the empty drinks stacked up around her. Still not beer, no matter how much it felt as though that would take away some of the pain she felt.

She needed to keep her mind sharp if she was going to see any kind of pattern in all of this.

Maya's eyes scanned over the case files for the tenth time, trying to find any connection beyond the Moonlight Serenade. She couldn't shake the feeling that there was something important she was missing, a clue that would tie everything together.

It felt as though she didn't have enough information, but Maya had everything she was likely to get from these two murders, the two that the Moonlight Killer had assured her that this serial killer had committed.

Except...

Maya froze as she realized the mistake she'd made. Frank Hanratty had never said that Rose Kallen and Emily Blackwell were the killer's only victims. He'd only said that there was more than one victim and confirmed that Emily was one of the victims. He *hadn't* said that there weren't more. But Maya had stopped looking once she'd found Emily.

She went back to the files she had access to, looking for murders up and down the East Coast. Emily's still stood out, but Maya kept looking, trying to filter through those that had happened in other ways, looking for women who had been strangled, then reading through the files to try to find ones that seemed to fit with the pattern.

At first, there was nothing, but slowly, Maya started to find them. Four, possibly five women, all up the coast, all found strangled not far from docks. Only the fact that they were in different towns and that the murders had taken place at different times had presumably stopped anyone from spotting that there was a serial killer at work before.

Yet all of the murders had taken place at docks, all of them at night, all of them targeting women.

Maya thought about what she'd realized about the murders of Rose Kallen and Emily Blackwell, too. She did her best to find the approximate times of death for all of the other murders, then ran them through the tide tracker that she'd found before online.

What she saw made her stop and stare at the screen. It wasn't just a weird coincidence anymore, it was a pattern: every single murder had taken place at high tide, at night. Not just at high tide, but at higher than usual tides. Rose Kallen's murder had been during a spring tide caused by the full moon, but the sun, the moon, air pressure, storm surges and more could all affect tides locally. Some combination of those factors had been in play with every murder.

A killer who only murdered his victims when the tide was high, higher than usual, and at night. The pattern was too obvious to ignore, and Maya felt her heart racing with excitement.

Maya sat back in her chair, trying to process everything she had just discovered. The killer wasn't just a random serial killer, and he wasn't trying to copy the Moonlight Killer's pattern; he had a specific type of victim and a specific time and place to strike. It was a calculated and premeditated plan, one that had gone unnoticed for far too long.

But she also felt frustration. Learning that pattern told her something about when the killer might strike again, and maybe hinted at where, but it didn't get Maya closer to knowing about the identity of the killer.

But maybe knowing about the additional victims might help her. Would Samit help her again? Maya didn't know, but she had to try.

She called him. He picked up after a few rings.

"Agent Gray..." Maya could hear the hesitation in his voice.

"Samit, I guess you've heard some of what happened?" Maya said.

"They're saying you're going off after your own obsession," Samit said.

"There are more murders, Samit. I think I've found four, maybe five. But to find the killer, I need-"

"I'm sorry, Maya," Samit said. "I can't give you anything else. If it's flagged after everything that happened, I could be fired. I could be"

"Lucy Barnet could be killed," Maya said. "I know how much I'm asking, Samit, but-"

"I'm sorry, Maya, I can't."

Samit hung up a moment later. It was obvious that he didn't want to be caught talking on an open line to an FBI agent who was on the verge of disgrace. Maya couldn't blame him for that. She didn't want to drag Samit down with her if she got fired.

But she *did* need to find this killer.

Maya could only work with the information she had, though. That meant the files on the murders, the information she had on the murders she'd just found, and the shipping manifests that she already had.

Those manifests only covered the dates of two of the murders, so Maya wasn't sure what good they would do. Especially when they'd already led her straight into a dead end.

The facts didn't change. The Moonlight Serenade continued to be the only vessel that had docked at both Ellonsea and Oakville. If Maya couldn't find a pattern that fit at least those two, then having the manifests for the other murders wouldn't help at all.

There were no ships that appeared on both, other than the Moonlight Serenade. No ships, but...

...what if it wasn't about the ships?

Maya realized the mistake that she'd made then. She'd been thinking about a ship going from place to place, carrying the killer, carrying a consistent crew, but that wasn't the way ship crews worked, was it? They shifted and changed. Some crew members would work a ship for years, but others would drift from vessel to vessel, picking up work wherever they could, traveling back and forth between favored locations.

What if the killer were taking advantage of that? What if he was deliberately drifting, hopping from boat to boat, knowing that it would help him to remain anonymous?

If that were true, then it meant that Maya shouldn't be looking for boats that had been in both places, but crew members.

Maya felt both a surge of worry and a hint of hope at that possibility. Hope, because it might give her a new lead on the killer's identity. Worry, because how could she possibly track down individual crew members from various vessels? Looking through the manifests to find crew members who had been in both locations felt as though it might take forever.

But she had to try.

Maya started poring over crew lists from various ships that had docked at both Ellonsea and Teaksville during the times of the murders. It was slow going, but Maya didn't give in. She compared every name she saw to those on the other list. It was a tedious task, but eventually she found a name that appeared on two manifests: Harlan Tompkinson.

Maya's heart began to race as she dug deeper into Tompkinson's background.

He had a criminal record, including a violent assault charge. It seemed that he drifted between ships, never staying on one for very long.

He hadn't been on the Moonlight Serenade, but he had been in Ellonsea on another cargo vessel on the night of Rose Kallen's murder. He'd been on what appeared to be a charter fishing boat that docked in Teaksville when Emily Blackwell died. He appeared to be a skipper for hire, captaining or piloting boats and then moving on. His name was right there on the manifests as captain.

Would it be anywhere else? Maya went back to the ship-tracking site she'd used before to track the Moonlight Serenade. Looking through the ship details, she saw that the captain's name was up there. She just hoped that it was a searchable feature.

It was, and Maya breathed a sigh of relief as she put in Harlan Tompkinson's name, checking which boat, if any, he was currently working on.

Maya discovered that Tompkinson was currently the captain of a cargo vessel called the Siren's Song, which was en route to a town called Callinport. It was a little further along the coast. She could drive it, but if she was wrong about this, there would be no time to do anything else before the midnight deadline.

Maya considered calling the information in. She had the name of a probable serial killer, and she could have cops waiting for him when he made landfall.

After everything that had happened, though, Maya knew that the police and FBI wouldn't believe her without solid evidence. They would look at what had happened with the Moonlight Serenade and see it as her crying wolf again. It was obvious that the whole of the FBI, even Marco, viewed Maya as acting out of obsession. They wouldn't believe what she had to say.

And she didn't have proof, not really. She had evidence that Tompkinson had been in the towns where the murders had taken place, but she didn't have anything that would tie him directly to either death.

She needed to catch Harlan Tompkinson in the act, red-handed, if she wanted to put him away for good. To do that, she would need to get to Callinport.

On instinct, Maya checked the tides around Callinport for the night, cross-checking them against the likely arrival time of the Siren's Song.

It would show up at high tide. At a *very* high tide, judging by the reports. That was both bad and good.

Bad, because, if Maya was right, it meant that Harlan Tompkinson would be hunting for a victim.

Good, because it gave Maya a chance to catch him in the act.

Maya grabbed her coat and headed for her car. She had to get to Callinport and find the Siren's Song before it was too late. The sun was setting, casting long shadows across the empty streets.

She made it back to the car and got inside, ready to start the long drive to the town where the killer was waiting. She would have to drive fast again, hoping that she was quick enough, hoping that she could make it to Callinport before Tompkinson made landfall and picked out another victim.

She was interrupted by a tap on the window. Maya froze, wondering if maybe the local cops were there, if she'd parked in the wrong place or something.

Instead, she looked up and saw Megan standing there.

CHAPTER TWENTY FOUR

"Megan, what are you doing here?" Maya said as she got out of the car. In spite of Marco's call earlier, she couldn't believe that her sister was there in Teaksville, that she'd come all the way here.

"You said where you were going and then I tracked your GPS." Megan countered. "Never mind that. What are *you* doing here, Maya?"

Maya hesitated, unsure of how to explain everything to her sister. She briefly considered lying, but she knew she couldn't keep the truth from Megan forever. "I'm working on a case," she said finally. "It's... complicated."

Megan looked at Maya skeptically. "A case? Maya, you're just obsessing over the same cases as before, aren't you? Marco told me that you're looking into the Rose Kallen murder?"

"Not just that," Maya said. Maya took a deep breath, gathering her thoughts. "There have been a series of murders along the coast," she said carefully. "I think they're all connected, and I'm trying to find the killer."

She didn't have time for this. She had to get moving, had to find Harlan Tompkinson before he killed again. But she knew her sister wouldn't let her go without an explanation.

"You've been looking at those fifteen cases for months now, trying to find ones that don't fit the Moonlight Killer's pattern. Now, you've latched onto this one, and you've decided that there's another killer out there."

"I know how this looks," Maya said. She knew that she'd alienated her sister by doing this, her fiance, the FBI. Maybe the kidnapper who had taken Lucy Barnet had intended that. Maybe, making Maya look like a crazy FBI agent who had gone off the rails was a part of his plan.

If so, it was working, and Maya still couldn't stop.

"Do you?" Megan asked. "Because it looks like you're obsessed, Maya. It looks like you've been obsessed ever since that night in the bunker."

Just the mention of it was enough to make Maya's blood run cold, and the memories that came flooding back were almost too much for her to bear.

In that moment, she could have been back there again, facing off against Frank Hanratty, watching as he dragged Megan out of there. She was back at his cabin, taking him down, saving Megan.

"You threw yourself into trying to catch his copycats and the people who helped him," Megan said. "And at first, I thought that was good. I thought you were making a difference. But now... now I see that you needed that, Maya. You needed to keep taking on the Moonlight Killer in some form. And since then, with your 'research' for the book? It was just a way to keep investigating this case."

"I'm not obsessed," Maya said firmly. "I'm just trying to do my job, to catch a killer."

Megan shook her head. "Maya, you need to let this go. This isn't a case you've been assigned. This is something you've decided to go after by yourself. You need to come home, Maya."

"I can't come back right now," Maya said. She checked the time. She would have to hurry if she was going to make it to Callinport in time.

"Maya, I'm here to take you home, and I'm not leaving without you. This has to stop."

Maya felt a surge of anger rise up in her chest, but she forced it down. She couldn't afford to waste time arguing with her sister. "I can't just let this go, Megan," she said. "There are lives at stake here."

"Lives at stake?" Megan repeated incredulously. "What lives? You don't even know if there's a killer out there, or if there is, whether it's the same one who killed Rose Kallen."

"I do," Maya said. "There is a serial killer making his way up the coast, killing women as he goes. I have a name for him and I believe I know where he will land next, at a town named Callinport. When he lands, I believe he will find someone to kill."

"Maya, I think that's a reach, and in any case, if you think you have found a killer, you should contact the local cops, or your colleagues at the FBI, or someone. You should get backup."

"I can't do that," Maya said.

"Because you've already messed up? Marco told me about the thing with the boat."

"Because Lucy Barnet will be killed if I don't see this through to the end!" Maya retorted. She couldn't hold it back anymore, couldn't keep this secret inside her.

Megan gave her a worried look. "What are you talking about?" she asked. "What does Lucy have to do with anything?"

"She went missing after the funeral. Marco didn't believe it. No one really did. Then I received a postcard."

Maya saw the horror that passed over Megan's face. She knew that her sister understood the implications of that.

"A postcard? From him?"

Maya shook her head, feeling a sudden wave of relief at being able to explain this to someone.

"Not from the Moonlight Killer. Someone else. Someone is trying to take over where he left off."

Megan's expression turned from horror to confusion. "What do you mean, take over where he left off?"

"They're using Lucy as leverage," Maya said. "They're forcing me to investigate the Rose Kallen murder, threatening to kill Lucy if I don't."

Megan looked like she was about to say something, but then her eyes widened in understanding. "That's why you're going to Callinport," she said. "You think that's where they're going to strike next."

Maya nodded, relieved that her sister was starting to understand. "Yes," she said. "I have reason to believe that Harlan Tompkinson, the man responsible for Rose Kallen's death, is planning to make landfall in Callinport tonight. And if he does, he'll find someone else to kill."

"And you can't tell the cops because..."

"Because he's playing by the same rules Frank Hanratty did," Maya said. "If I try to find the kidnapper, or if I bring in the rest of the FBI, Lucy dies. If I don't find answers by midnight tonight, if I don't catch the killer, she dies."

"So you're trying to do this all by yourself?" Megan said. "You didn't even tell Marco? You didn't feel as though you could tell *me*?"

"I wanted to keep you out of this," Maya said. "After everything you went through, I didn't want you to drag you back into something like this, especially after the way you reacted at Imogen's funeral."

"That was because I thought you were becoming consumed with obsession," Megan said. "I thought that you were dragging me back there. This... this is different. It's happening again, and you need to stop this. *We* need to stop this."

Megan, you can't come with me. It's too dangerous."

"I don't care," Megan said, her voice firm. "You need backup, Maya. And besides, I can't just let you go off on some crazy mission by yourself."

Maya felt a surge of gratitude for her sister, but she couldn't let her put herself in danger. Maya was a trained FBI agent and a former Military Intelligence officer. Megan was a civilian, an art student.

"I don't know," she said finally. "It's risky, Megan. I don't want to put you in danger."

"I'm a grown woman, Maya," Megan reminded her. "And I'm not going to let you face this alone. So tell me what you need me to do."

Maya took a deep breath, feeling a sense of relief wash over her. She hadn't realized how alone she'd been feeling, how much she'd needed someone to talk to. "Okay," she said. "I need to get to Callinport. Time is running out."

Maya got into the car. Megan started to go around to the passenger side door, but Maya locked it before she could get there.

"Maya? What are you doing? Maya?"

Maya put the car in gear and started to drive, heading for Callinport. She had to finish this, and she wasn't about to risk Megan's life while she did.

Maya sped towards Callinport, driving as fast as she dared in the growing dark. Her phone started to ring, with Megan's name appearing on the screen. Maya answered it, and quickly regretted it.

"Maya, what do you think you're doing? You can't just abandon me like this. You-"

"I'm sorry, Megan, but I can't put you in danger."

Maya hung up and kept driving.

She kept an eye on the time as she drove. It would take her at least a couple of hours to get to Callinport, maybe longer, and it was already getting late. Maya didn't know if she was going to make it there before Harlan Tompkinson made landfall, and, if so, if she was going to be able to stop him from killing again.

Maya could feel the weight of the situation press upon her shoulders, the lives of innocent women all depending on her success. She couldn't let herself think about the possibility of failure. She had to succeed. She couldn't afford to let anyone else die. She had to stop this killer before he struck again. But how? She didn't have any leads, any ideas on where to start. All she knew was that he was heading to Callinport and that he was going to kill someone once he got there.

As Maya drove, she caught a glimpse of the sea off to her right. She saw the waves crashing against the shore and the moonlight reflecting off the water. For a moment, she felt a sense of calm wash over her. It was as if the ocean was telling her that everything was going to be okay, that she could do this.

Then, suddenly, the calm was gone. Maya realized that she was running out of time. She had to act fast if she was going to stop this killer. She took a deep breath and tried to think. What could she do?

Then, a thought occurred to her. She reached for her phone and dialed a number.

"Hello?" Samit's voice answered.

"Samit," Maya said. "It's Maya. I need your help."

There was a pause on the other end of the line.

"What kind of help? I already told you that I can't-"

"I'm not asking you to get me more information or anything like that. I just need you to make one phone call for me at a particular time."

"And you can't make that call yourself?" Samit asked.

"I could," Maya said, "but I suspect that at that time, I'll be in the middle of taking down a serial killer."

Maya told him exactly what she needed, and Samit hesitated on the other end of the line.

"All right," he said at last. "I'll do it. Be careful, Agent Gray."

Maya couldn't promise him that. All she could do was hang up, push the gas pedal to the floor, and hope that she got to Callinport in time to stop Harlan Tompkinson.

CHAPTER TWENTY FIVE

Harlan stared ahead as he piloted the Siren's Song, guiding it towards Callinport. It was getting closer by the moment, and Harlan could feel the tension rising in him.

Rising like the tide that carried the small cargo vessel towards the port. The tide was higher than it should have been, the moon shining down on the waves through gaps in the clouds above, rain falling steadily.

Harlan knew what that meant, what he would have to do when he landed.

The thought of that made him grip the ship's wheel tighter, gritting his teeth against the wind and the rain. Harlan's eyes were hidden behind his glasses, shaggy brown hair covering the side of his face. His pale skin was covered in droplets of water, both rain and sweat. His jaw was tense, his mouth a thin line. Harlan was in his mid-forties, with a broken nose and a perpetual scowl.

He wasn't a man who made friends easily. It was one of the reasons that he drifted from ship to ship, never staying in a job for long. The other reason...

...well, it meant that no one learned too much about him. No one learned the things that he did on nights like this.

Harlan had a length of rope in the pocket of his windbreaker. He had to stop himself from reaching for it. It wouldn't come to that. He wouldn't have to kill someone tonight.

He wasn't sure whether that thought made him feel hopeful or disappointed. A part of him was reveling in this, in the storm boosting the tide, in the prospect of the kill.

Harlan hated that part of himself. It was a part that had been there as long as he could remember, a part that he'd managed to push down. That part of himself, he was sure, was the reason why he was cursed.

Once, he wouldn't have believed in such things. Once, he had laughed at old sailors' superstitions. But not anymore. Not after he had lost everything. If he weren't cursed, why would the ocean have claimed Margaritte, the high tide swallowing her, taking her into its depths, pulling her under?

It was impossible to think of her now without pain. Harlan's tears joined the raindrops on his face, spilling down his cheeks.

He wiped them away quickly, his resolve hardening. He couldn't let himself get distracted. Not now. He had a task to do if he was going to avoid killing someone tonight.

Harlan looked out towards the port, his eyes scanning the area. He could see the lights of the town in the distance, and he could make out the shapes of the buildings.

The harbor office would have a tide clock. Harlan could see it in the distance, making out the shape of the building, already plotting his route to it.

Harlan wasn't sure how he had settled on tide clocks, except that a thing that measured an event always seemed inextricably linked to it, to have a kind of control. What Harlan *did* know was that if he reached a tide clock there before he saw a woman, he wouldn't have to hurt anyone. He could let out all the awful tension inside him, rest up for the night and get ready to head out again on another ship.

If he saw a woman, though... then he would have no choice. It would be a sign from Margaritte that she wanted another soul to join her. He would have to stalk her, have to strangle her, as he had the others. He would have to unleash that savage part of himself to kill.

He guided the ship into the port. The Siren's Song rocked violently as Harlan fought to keep control of the ship. The wind howled, making it difficult for him to hear any other sounds.

The ship slowly drew to a halt by the docks. The rest of the crew were waiting to tie it off and unload it. Harlan didn't care about any of that, not then.

He stood at the top of the gangway, making sure that he was ahead of any of them, making sure that he was looking down so that he wouldn't meet the gaze of any women as he started to make his way into the town.

Harlan moved quickly, determined to get to the harbor office and the tide clock that would be waiting there. If he could do that, everything would be all right for another voyage, no matter how much the other part of him insisted that he should go looking for a victim, that he should stalk one, and kill her, that he should...

Harlan was so lost in his thoughts that he barely noticed the approaching figure until they bumped into him, making him stumble.

"Sorry, sorry," a voice said.

Harlan looked up and found himself staring at a woman. At the woman he would kill tonight.

CHAPTER TWENTY SIX

Maya reeled back from the impact of bumping into Harlan Tompkinson, trying to make herself look a little unsteady on her feet, like she was drunk or drugged, or both.

Like she was a victim.

Maya had spent most of the drive over to Callinsport contemplating what she would do once she got there. Now, she was in the town, and the moment had come to put her plan into action.

She *could* simply have arrested him the moment he arrived in the port, but then what? She didn't have any physical proof to tie him to the murders, only the circumstantial evidence of the timing and his presence in the towns.

After the mistake Maya had made with the Moonlight Serenade, there was no way that anyone would believe her based on that now. She would be relying on Harlan confessing, on getting him to incriminate himself when she questioned him.

Maya couldn't rely on that. There was every chance that he would stay silent, lawyer up. Even if she managed to find other evidence on him or wear him down until he talked, that would come too late for Lucy Barnet. The kidnapper's deadline would pass, and Lucy would die.

Maya needed to take Harlan down before that, and she needed proof that he was the killer Maya knew him to be. That meant... that meant that she had to get him to try to kill her.

She had to make him see her as a victim first. She had to make him let his guard down. And that meant playing a dangerous game of cat and mouse.

Maya looked up at Harlan, her eyes wide and innocent, fluttering her eyelashes in a way she hoped was convincing.

"Oh, I'm so sorry," she slurred her words a bit, swaying on her feet. "I didn't see you there."

Harlan looked down at her, his eyes narrowing behind his glasses. He looked almost remorseful, standing there like he didn't want to do this. Remorseful, but also hungry, eager, at the same time, like there was some other side to him that wanted this.

"Are you all right?" Harlan asked, sounding almost concerned.

"I'm fine," Maya said, forcing a smile. "Just a little tipsy. I was at a party. Sorry, I should go."

She staggered off along the street, using reflections in windowpanes to look behind her, hoping that this would work.

Sure enough, Maya saw the reflection of someone behind her, following. Maya didn't look around to check. It was enough to know that Harlan was following her, that he intended for her to be his prey.

Maya quickened her pace, turning a corner and walking down a dimly lit alley, hoping that she could lead Harlan deeper into the town. He thought he was hunting her, but in reality, she was the one hunting him, leading him forward into a trap that would prove he was the killer beyond a doubt.

She had already picked out the spot where she wanted this to end, in a small plaza not far from the dock offices. There would be no one there at this time of night, and Maya had no doubt that Harlan would be happy to try to kill her there. After all, he'd had no problem killing Emily Blackwell right outside a similar office.

Maya kept going, trying to judge her pace correctly. Too slow, and Harlan might catch up to her before she was ready for him. Too fast, and he might fall behind and lose her.

She needed to make sure that he was fully committed to the chase, that he was convinced that she was his prey, and that there was no turning back from what was about to happen.

Maya took twists and turns. She didn't know this city, but she'd looked at maps of the place while she was waiting for the ship to arrive, and she knew the general direction she was aiming for.

The worrying thing was that Maya couldn't hear Harlan's footsteps behind her anymore, or see any sign of him. She cursed to herself, but kept walking, retracing some of her steps as if lost. She could only hope that he was out there somewhere, watching her. That he hadn't given up and gone off to try to kill someone else.

All Maya could do was go back along her route, continuing to look as vulnerable as she could, and hoping that Harlan wanted her dead.

As she walked, Maya thought about how the kidnapper would know if she had succeeded in this. The Moonlight Killer had tapped into her phone. Would this new kidnapper have done the same, or would he just be listening in to police and FBI channels?

Would he even care? This was a different kidnapper with different aims. Maya had no guarantee that he would even let her go, that he wouldn't just kill Lucy anyway. Maya was taking it on trust that he was going to do this the same way the Moonlight Killer would.

She tried to force herself not to think about it. Right now, she had to concentrate on Harlan. She had to catch him, whatever happened afterwards. This was a serial killer, one who would only keep killing women if Maya didn't stop him.

It was hard not to look around too often, not to give away that she knew that he was out there somewhere, that she knew exactly what he was. Had Maya spooked him? If he guessed that she was FBI, if he worked out that she was hunting him, then there was a chance that he might run, and she would never catch him in time.

So she kept walking, kept trying to look vulnerable, kept trying to draw him in. Maya used reflections to try to look for any hint of him.

She was almost relieved when she heard footsteps behind her again, when she caught the flicker of a shadow that shouldn't have been there. She had to remind herself not to let that relief show on her face as she went back on her circuitous route towards the plaza.

Maya was halfway there when she heard the footsteps getting closer, and she felt a hint of fear then, in spite of being the one to set this situation up. She'd walked into danger with her eyes open, but the danger was still there.

Maya kept walking towards the plaza, but Harlan was closing in now. Maya guessed that he would catch up to her just as she reached a spot where the alley she was in widened, under a streetlight.

It wasn't far enough. Maya's call to Samit had been to get him to arrange backup, and she'd already picked the spot where that backup would be waiting.

Maya couldn't just run for the plaza, though, couldn't risk having Harlan at her back any longer. Instead, she stood under the street light and turned in place, ready to confront him.

Harlan emerged from the shadows, his face twisted with a mix of desire and anger. Maya could see the hunger in his eyes, the same hunger that had driven him to kill all those innocent women.

"What do you want?" she asked, trying not to let her fear show.

"It's not about what I want," Harlan said. He had a length of rope in his hand. "It's about what has to happen. Do you think I want to do this?"

"I think, with all the women you've killed, there must be some part of you that wants this," Maya said.

Harlan looked at her in surprise. "How... how did you know? Who *are* you?"

"My name is Agent Maya Gray, with the FBI." There was no point in holding that back now that Harlan had admitted it. "Why don't you put down the rope and give yourself up?"

"I can't," Harlan said. He winced. "This has to happen. I saw you before I could get to a tide clock. You were the first I saw. You have to die. You have to!"

"I'm FBI, Harlan. This isn't going to work."

"It doesn't matter," Harlan replied. "It doesn't matter who you are or what you do. What you think you're *going* to do. All that matters is that you were the one I saw. I saw you, and now you have to die."

Harlan lunged at Maya, the rope clutched in his hands.

CHAPTER TWENTY SEVEN

Maya flung herself to the side, dodging Harlan's attack, her training kicking in as she blocked his blows. She knew that she was the only one standing between this monster and the safety of countless other women.

Harlan was stronger than she expected, but Maya was faster, using her agility to evade his attacks and strike back with precision. She landed a punch to his jaw, causing him to stumble back.

"Stop this, Harlan," Maya said, her voice firm. "It's over. You're going to jail for the rest of your life."

Harlan sneered, lunging at her again, but this time she was ready. She sidestepped his attack and delivered a swift kick to his kneecap, sending him stumbling to the ground.

Maya went to draw her gun then, determined to control the situation. Harlan whipped the rope around at her, its knotted end snapping into her hand. It didn't make Maya lose her grip, but it did mean that when her gun went off, the bullet went wide. The sound of the shot echoed through the alleyway.

The miss gave Harlan all the time that he needed. He lunged at Maya again, grabbing for her gun arm and twisting, wrapping the rope around it as he kept the weapon pointed away from him.

Maya struggled to break free, but Harlan was too strong. She could feel the rope tightening around her wrist, cutting off her circulation. Harlan wrenched her arm with painful, almost breaking, force, so that the only way for Maya to avoid injury was to let go of the gun. It went clattering to the ground. She used her free hand to punch him in the face, and he staggered back, releasing her arm.

Harlan's weight slammed into her as he charged her, knocking her to the ground. Maya landed on her back, the air knocked out of her lungs. Harlan straddled her, his hands closing around her throat. She struggled to breathe as he squeezed, trying to choke the life out of her.

Panic surged through Maya's body, but she didn't give up. She fought with all her strength, clawing at Harlan's face, trying to pry his grip loose. Desperation fueled her as her vision began to blur. She couldn't let this be how it ended.

With a sudden burst of energy, Maya managed to buck Harlan off of her. She scrambled to her feet, gasping for air.

Maya struck at him with the heel of her hand, hit him with a knee, punched him in the guts, anything to wear him down and take the fight out of him. None of it seemed to be working.

Her eyes fell on the discarded gun, only a few feet away. Maya lunged for it, determined to get to it.

She was too slow. Harlan caught her with a kick to the side of the head that made Maya see stars. It stunned her, leaving her trying to push her way back to her feet, trying to get to the gun. Something.

Even as she did it, Maya saw the flash of the rope in front of her. Too late, she realized what Harlan was doing. Maya managed to get a couple of fingers between it and her neck, but even so, she felt the crushing pressure of it as it bit into her throat.

Now, Maya felt Harlan's strength. This was a man who had worked on boats his whole life, moving cargo, hauling on ropes. Hard, physical work. It felt as though Maya's head was going to be wrenched off her shoulders.

Maya's vision began to tunnel as she struggled to wrestle the rope from around her neck. She could hear the sound of Harlan's laughter, muffled by the ringing in her ears. Panic set in as she realized that she might not make it out of this alive.

She found herself thinking about Marco, who didn't even know what she was doing here but would be broken at the loss of her. She thought of Lucy Barnet, whose life depended on Maya's survival here, on her taking down Harlan. She thought about Megan, who would know where Maya had gone, who might blame herself for this, for not stopping Maya from coming to Callinsport alone.

Maya kept fighting, kept trying to break free. Maya's vision was going dark, and panic set in. She knew that this could be the end. She couldn't breathe, couldn't think, could only feel the rope tightening around her throat. She clawed at the rope, trying to find a way to loosen the pressure.

That was when Maya saw Megan, running towards her and Harlan. Maya assumed that she was imagining it, that her oxygen-starved brain was conjuring up dreams of the people she cared about.

Then Megan hit Harlan, her full weight behind the blow, sending him tumbling from Maya's back, the rope coming away from her throat as he fell away.

Maya gasped for air, barely able to believe what had just happened. Megan had saved her. Maya saw Harlan's face contort with rage as he turned to face her sister. For a moment, he seemed to forget about Maya altogether, his focus now on Megan. He moved to attack her.

Maya scrambled to her feet, her fingers still rubbing at her bruised throat as she watched Harlan advance on Megan. Her sister was smaller, weaker, and more vulnerable than Maya was, and she couldn't bear the thought of her being hurt.

Maya's anger boiled over as she faced Harlan, adrenaline coursing through her veins. She kicked Harlan hard, knocking him back away from Megan.

As he turned towards Maya, Megan hit out at him, the two of them working in concert now to try to take on the killer. Harlan turned back towards Megan, lashing out at her, catching her with a punch.

Maya scrambled forwards, the adrenaline pumping through her veins as she saw Harlan lunging at her sister. She couldn't let him hurt Megan. Not after everything that had happened. Not after everything they had been through.

Maya tackled Harlan from the side, slamming him into the wall. He grunted as the air was knocked from his lungs. Maya punched him in the face, her fist connecting with bone. Harlan staggered back, his eyes flashing with anger as he tried to regain his balance.

Maya didn't give him the chance. She kicked out with her foot, hitting him in the stomach. Harlan doubled over, and Maya followed up with a powerful uppercut that sent him sprawling to the ground.

Harlan turned and ran then, heading off along the alleyway.

"How... how did you..." Maya managed.

"You told me where you were going," Megan said. "And I followed you while you led that guy, trying to get him to attack you. Do you know how dangerous that is, Maya? You abandoned me back in Teaksville."

"I just wanted you to be safe," Maya said.

"And put *yourself* in danger," Megan shot back. She gestured in the direction Harlan had run. "Shouldn't we be chasing him?"

It would have been so easy to let him go. The pain of her bruises and the need to gasp in air both demanded it, but if Maya did that, she wouldn't catch him in time. If he got away, Lucy was going to die.

Snatching up her gun, she forced herself to chase after Harlan. Megan ran along with her, the two of them trying to catch up to the killer before he could get away.

Maya could feel the burn in her lungs as she ran. She was still recovering from being strangled, but right now, her adrenaline was pumping. She'd rarely been so focused on anything before.

Harlan, in his desperation, was taking twists and turns. Maya and Megan kept running after him, following him around every corner.

Maya could hear the sounds of police sirens in the distance, becoming louder. She didn't know how long they had before the police arrived, but she suspected that they wouldn't be in time to help with this.

The streets of Callinsport were deserted as they ran, the rain and the late hour keeping people inside. Maya and Megan chased Harlan through the alleyways and backstreets. They could hear the sound of his footsteps pounding the pavement, the echo of his breathing, and the rustle of his clothing as he ran.

Harlan took another turn then, briefly disappearing from view. Maya and Megan followed him, Megan putting on a burst of speed as if she wanted to make sure that she was the first one to him.

Maya heard her cry out even as she rounded the corner. Maya saw Harlan there, his rope around her sister's neck, already pulled tight.

Maya's heart sank at the sight of her sister in such a perilous position. She raised her gun, aiming it at Harlan.

"Let her go, Harlan," she said, her voice low and threatening. "Or I'll shoot."

Harlan didn't seem to care.

"You've ruined everything," he said. "Both of you. Don't you know how much damage you've caused?"

"As much as you?" Maya replied. She was looking for a clear shot, but Harlan was keeping Megan between him and her. Megan was scrabbling at the rope around her neck, her face turning red as Harlan strangled her.

"Let my sister go, Harlan."

"Let me go," Harlan said. "Let me go, and I'll let her go."

Megan shook her head even as Harlan strangled her. Maya knew what she meant: they couldn't let him get away with Lucy's life at stake.

"Let her go, or I'll shoot," Maya said, still looking for a shot.

You won't do it," he said, his voice mocking. "You're not going to shoot through your own sister to get to me."

Maya's finger tightened on the trigger. She knew that he was right - she wasn't going to shoot through her sister. But she also knew that she couldn't let him hurt Megan, or get away.

Maya aimed carefully, her heart beating quickly after the chase, her ragged breath making it hard to keep the barrel of the Glock steady.

"Megan, drop!" she shouted.

Megan went limp, dropping her full weight from the rope. For an instant, Maya had a clear shot. She pulled the trigger. The shot rang out in the empty alleyway, striking Harlan in the shoulder. Harlan cried out, and his grip on Megan loosened. She fell to the ground, gasping for air.

Maya wanted to run to her sister, but Harlan was the threat. She had to make sure that he couldn't hurt anyone else. She went to him, forcing him over onto his stomach and cuffing him.

Megan stood, gasping for breath. Megan was trembling, but she seemed to be okay.

"Thank you," Megan said.

Even as she said it, cops started to pour into the alleyway they were in, their guns drawn ready to deal with any trouble. Maya held up her badge. She wanted to be clear what was happening here.

"FBI. The situation is under control, and that man, Harlan Tompkinson, is under arrest for murder."

Maya just hoped that it would be enough to save Lucy Barnet's life.

CHAPTER TWENTY EIGHT

Maya stepped out of the interrogation room, breathing a sigh of relief. Megan was waiting out there, the bruises on her throat already blooming. Maya was sure that she had a set to match them on her own throat.

"Harlan is talking," Maya said.

"What's he saying?" Megan asked, sounding anxious.

"He's admitting to everything," Maya replied. "He killed Rose Kallen and the other women. He's confessed to... he apparently needed to find a tide clock before he saw a woman every time he landed on a very high tide, and if not, he had to kill her."

"That... that's insane," Megan said.

"*He's* insane, probably," Maya replied. "It doesn't matter right now. What matters is that we caught him."

Megan let out a shuddering breath. "Thank god."

Maya nodded. "Yeah, it's over now. We can finally bring closure to their families and bring Harlan to justice."

"And Lucy?"

That was the question that hung over all of this, the one that mattered. Maya had only been investigating this case because Lucy Barnet had been taken by an unknown kidnapper, and he'd been holding the threat of killing her over Maya.

"Maya, is this going to get Lucy back safely?" Megan asked.

Maya hesitated for a moment before responding. "We're still waiting for the kidnapper to release her. But with Harlan in custody, we're hoping that the kidnapper doesn't have any reason to harm her."

Megan nodded, her expression a mix of relief and worry. "I hope so. I can't imagine what Lucy is going through. No, worse than that. I *can* imagine it because I've been there."

She had. She'd been held by the Moonlight Killer for months while he forced Maya to investigate case after case. She would know exactly what it was like, being held, knowing that she might die if Maya failed, hoping, believing that she would succeed but knowing the price if she didn't.

"It will be all right," Maya said. She wanted to believe that. She wanted to believe that the kidnapper would make contact soon to let them know where Lucy was.

"It's after midnight," Megan pointed out.

They both knew the significance of that. After midnight, after the deadline that the killer had set. They'd taken Harlan down before then, but did the kidnapper know that? Did he care?

It was hard to push down the fear that Maya felt then. Hard for her to let go of the possibility that Lucy Barnet might already be dead, either because the kidnapper thought that Maya had failed to meet his deadline, or because that had been his plan all along.

Had it been? This wasn't the Moonlight Killer. For all Maya knew, the whole point of this had been to make her jump through the kidnapper's hoops, only for Lucy to die anyway. He'd only kidnapped her, after all, for this one investigation. He didn't need Maya to *keep* investigating, which meant that he didn't need Lucy anymore.

Maya's phone buzzed in her pocket, interrupting her thoughts. She pulled it out and saw an unfamiliar number.

"Hello?" she answered cautiously.

"Agent Gray?" a voice on the other end asked.

"Yes, this is Agent Gray. Who is this?" Maya asked, her heart racing.

"You don't need to know that," the voice on the other end of the phone said. "What you *do* need to know is the location of Lucy Barnet."

Maya looked around, trying to find any cops who might be able to help her, maybe trace the call. There was no one there who looked like they could do anything, but maybe she could get Samit to trace it afterwards.

The kidnapper seemed to know what she was thinking.

"This is a burner phone, and by the time you trace the location, I'll be gone. Now listen."

He started to reel off a string of numbers. Maya realized that they were coordinates. She took out a pen, writing them on a scrap of paper, wanting to make sure that she got them all down.

"Did you get all that?" the kidnapper asked. "I hope so. Lucy Barnet's life depends on it. I doubt she'll have long."

He hung up.

Maya thought about calling Samit to try to get a trace on the call, but the kidnapper had already told her how useless that would be.

Unless she could pull satellite imaging to track him from the spot where his phone could be traced, it wouldn't get anywhere. And if he'd already pulled the SIM card and destroyed it, they wouldn't even get a trace.

Finding the kidnapper wasn't the priority right then. Getting Lucy Barnet back safely was.

Maya put the string of coordinates into an online map, hoping to turn it into a location. It gave her one, near DC. Near home.

But not near Callinsport. It would take hours to drive back there, even at the kinds of speeds Maya had been pushing herself to in this investigation.

She thought of the ways the Moonlight Killer had returned women to Maya in the past. He'd left them in precarious situations, either exposed to the elements or tied in places where rising water would eventually drown them. Recovering them had always been time-critical, and Maya didn't know if she could get to Lucy in time. She needed another option.

She could call this into the FBI directly, but Maya wasn't sure if anyone would even believe her right then. There would be a lot of questions to answer, and it would take time to convince them. Maya wasn't sure if Lucy Barnet had that kind of time left.

Besides, there was one person Maya trusted far more: Marco.

Maya called him.

"Maya?" Marco answered the phone groggily.

"Marco, it's me," Maya said urgently. "I need your help."

"Maya, where are you?" Marco asked. "Are you still in Teaksville? I thought Megan was bringing you home."

"I'm in a town called Callinsport," Maya said. "But that's not important right now. What matters is that Lucy Barnet's been located, but it's not near Callinsport. I need you to get there as fast as you can."

"Lucy Barnet?" Marco said, clearly not understanding. "Maya, what does you going after the Rose Kallen case have to do with Lucy?"

"There was... there was a postcard, Marco."

"A postcard?" Marco's voice was filled with confusion. "Maya, what the hell are you talking about?"

"A postcard left for me, just like before. Just like with the Moonlight Killer cases. Either I solved Rose Kallen's murder by midnight tonight or..."

"Or Lucy died," Marco finished. "That's... Maya, why didn't you tell me any of this?"

"You were on a case," Maya said. "And I thought you would want to bring in the rest of the FBI. If you did that, they would start hunting for the kidnapper, just like last time, and the kidnapper would kill her. But now, I have a location for her and I'm too far away from her to make sure that she's safe."

"So you're only bringing me in on this because you have to?" Marco said.

"Marco, Lucy is in danger."

"Okay, okay," Marco said, his voice more focused now. "Where is she? What do you need me to do?"

Maya told him the coordinates, and she could hear Marco typing, putting them into a computer.

"Okay," he said. "I have a location. I'll find her."

*

"She'll be fine," the doctor said, as he finished checking out Lucy Barnet.

Maya breathed a sigh of relief at that. After everything she'd been through, it was a miracle that Lucy had made it out alive.

"Can I talk to her?" Maya asked the doctor.

"Of course," he said. "She's been through a lot, so just take it easy on her."

Maya nodded, grateful for the chance to talk to Lucy. She walked into the hospital room, taking in the sight of Lucy lying in the bed, her eyes closed.

"Lucy?" Maya said softly.

Lucy's eyes opened, and she focused on Maya.

"Maya?" Lucy said weakly. "Is it over?"

"It's over," Maya said, a lump forming in her throat. "You're safe now."

Lucy let out a shuddering breath, tears filling her eyes.

"I thought I was going to die," she said. "He was going to kill me. Even when he took me and left me, I thought I was going to die out there."

He'd left Lucy staked out in a field. If Marco hadn't found her, she would have died from thirst or exposure.

"I'm glad Marco got to you in time," Maya said.

Lucy reached up to hug her. "He wouldn't have known where to find me without you."

Maya let the truth of that sink in for a moment. She'd done this. She'd gotten Lucy back safely by solving Rose Kallen's murder, and managed to get a serial killer off the streets at the same time.

Even so, Maya had questions.

"Lucy, what do you remember about the man who took you?"

"He didn't wear a mask," Lucy said. "It was like he didn't care if I saw his face. He was different to Hanratty, too. Not as weird. Almost normal."

"What about where he kept you?" Maya said.

"I don't know where it was. He drugged me to take me there, and again when he took me out."

So he'd been careful about that, but not about stopping Lucy from seeing his face. That was strange. Still, at least they had a chance of finding this kidnapper, working out who he was.

Maya was still thinking about that when Megan came into the hospital room. She hurried over and hugged Lucy. There were tears on her face.

"Oh, Lucy, we were so worried about you," Megan said. "I'm so glad you're okay."

"Thanks to Maya," Lucy said, and Maya felt a sense of pride at the gratitude in Lucy's voice.

Maya left the two of them there alone in the hospital room. If anyone understood what Lucy was going through, it was Megan. Maya suspected that if anyone could help Lucy to get through this, it was Megan.

Marco was waiting for Maya outside the hospital. Given everything that had happened since she'd last seen him, Maya couldn't help rushing forward to wrap her arms around him.

Marco held her tightly for a moment, but then pulled back.

"Maya, what the hell have you been doing the last couple of days?"

"Chasing a killer," Maya said. "I told you, Marco, there was a postcard. I didn't have a choice."

"You had a choice about who you included in this," Marco said. He looked hurt. "You didn't trust me enough to tell me what was going on. You didn't trust me enough to include me in this, even though I helped you with all of the Moonlight Killer cases."

"You were undercover on another case," Maya pointed out.

"Bullshit. If you really believed that would stop me from helping, you wouldn't have called me when you needed help to find Lucy."

Marco sounded angry now.

"Marco, I didn't want to put you in that position. We couldn't tell the rest of the FBI, and if they found out, *when* they found out, you might have lost your job."

"And that would have been my choice for getting involved," Marco said. "But you didn't *give* me the choice. I was with you on the whole hunt for the Moonlight Killer. I helped you keep the details of it from the rest of the FBI. I could have helped you on this."

"I couldn't take the risk," Maya said. "I know I should have, but-"

"But you wanted to do this alone," Marco said, cutting her off.

"You hadn't believed me about Lucy," Maya shot back.

"I would have believed you once the postcard arrived," Marco replied. He was obviously still angry. In fact, it looked like only an effort of will was keeping him there, keeping him from walking off. "This wasn't about me not believing you. This was about you not trusting me enough to include me in your plan. Or about wanting to be the hero, to get away from your desk job."

“This isn’t about my job,” Maya said. “And I’m not the one who goes away on undercover work all the time.”

“That’s my job,” Marco said. “And don’t think I can’t see that it hurts you, sitting behind a desk when you’d rather be out in the field.”

“Lucy would have died if I got the FBI involved.”

"If someone tried to find her," Marco corrected Maya. "I wouldn't have done that. I would have been by your side, helping you the way I always do."

Maya felt a pang of guilt. Marco was right, she should have trusted him enough to tell him everything. She'd been so focused on solving the case herself that she hadn't even considered how her actions might affect those around her.

"I'm sorry," Maya said softly. "I should have trusted you more, and I should have included you in everything."

"Maya, you've been obsessed for months, but the real obsession hasn't been the Moonlight Killer or the cases that might not be his. It's been an obsession with you being the only one who can make a difference, with you having to go off alone to solve everything. That has to stop. You have to include me, or... or what's the point of my even being here?"

He walked off then, leaving Maya feeling miserable. She'd messed up, and she'd hurt Marco in the process. She didn't know how to make it right, how to fix things between them. All she could do was try to do better in the future.

CHAPTER TWENTY NINE

Frank Hanratty sat in the back of the prison transport, watching the moonlight above through the small window. It was a full moon tonight, and that was always a moment that spoke to him.

Right now, though, he was more interested in the guards in the front of the van talking. There were two of them, one older, looking like he'd been on the job for years, one young and impatient.

"Why are we transporting him at this time of night?" the younger one asked.

"Beats me," the older one replied. "But Administrator Higgins says that an urgent transfer order has come through. Something about the risk of him being broken out. He says this one has come straight through from the FBI."

"The FBI are putting through transfer orders now?" the younger one asked.

"Not the order, idiot. The information that led to it. Probably came straight through from that Agent Gray who put him away."

Frank smiled at that thought. These men really thought that Maya would have him moved like this? That she'd been worried about him escaping, so she'd decided to get him sent to another prison in the dead of night? Did they think that Maya even had the power to do that?

No, that wasn't what was happening at all.

Frank sat there, waiting, trying to judge the passage of time by the movement of the moon across the sky. He was good at small skills like that, the kinds of things that a man might need to survive in a hostile world.

He used other cues to give him a sense of where the prison truck was. He could guess now at how far they'd come, and he already knew the route they would be taking.

Not that he *should* know. Prison transports varied their routes, deliberately trying to make it hard for anyone to interfere with their work. But the route had been set at the same time the order was put through, and that meant that Frank knew every detail.

It was time.

Frank crouched in the back of the transport, working quickly on his shackles with a couple of lock picks pulled from the lining of his socks, carefully pushed in there so that the guards wouldn't find them when they searched him. The shackles had actually done some good there, helping to hide the metal when they waved a metal detector over him.

He managed to free himself just as the transport slowed down, approaching a junction. Frank waited, still and quiet, bracing himself.

The moment when the truck slammed into the side of the prisoner transport was still jarring, the impact sending the transport spinning. The two guards were thrown around in the front of the vehicle like puppets being moved by some giant hand. Even braced as he was, Frank struggled to avoid being flung around in the same way.

The transport vehicle skidded to a stop. The two guards groaned, but started to recover. Even as they did so, Frank heard the sound of footsteps approaching the rear of the vehicle, heard the sound of preparations being made there.

Frank moved back from the doors with his hands over his ears just as his rescuer detonated the shaped charge that he'd put in place there. The sound of the explosion filled the vehicle, almost deafening him even though he was prepared for it. The doors swung open and Frank leapt down, out of the transport vehicle.

Even as stunned as they were, the guards were moving to intercept him. The younger one was staggering out of the truck, trying to reach for his gun.

"Get your hands up!" the guard yelled.

Frank was already moving in to meet him. He got his hands on the younger guard's wrist, stopping him from drawing the gun even as Frank's forehead slammed into the guard's face. That stunned him enough that Frank was able to wrench the gun clear, taking control of the weapon.

The older guard came around the side of the truck with a shotgun in his hands. He fired, but he was still so disoriented by the impact of the truck into the transport vehicle, and the shot went wide.

Frank's shots didn't. He fired three times, putting one round into the guard's head, two into his chest. The man collapsed, surprise on his face at the speed with which it had happened.

Frank turned to his savior. Administrator Higgins was standing there, dressed in dark clothes, but still wearing his glasses.

"Everything went according to plan with Lucy Barnet?" Frank asked.

"I released her as you said, once Agent Gray got the answer right. How did *you* know the identity of the killer?"

"Did you doubt that I would?" Frank asked.

The administrator looked momentarily scared. He'd helped Frank with all of this, done exactly what was required, but Frank had no doubt that he knew just how violently Frank would react to an insult.

"Is everything in place?" Frank asked.

Administrator Higgins nodded. "The bunker is ready. Everything else is exactly the way you demanded it should be. I've contacted the… others you told me about. They will be on their way."

The others. People who owed him. People who were like him, in some cases, or merely useful in others. People who would do exactly what he asked of them, because they were afraid of him, or admired him, or both. The way the administrator had done.

"Then let's get going," Frank said. "Just one thing first."

The younger guard was staggering away from the transport vehicle, obviously trying to get to some kind of safety. Maybe trying to get somewhere that he could call for help. Frank didn't give him a chance. He lifted his gun and fired once, shooting the guard in the back. He crumpled to the ground.

"Now we can go," he said. "We have a lot to do."

A lot to do, even now. Frank had been putting this in place almost from the moment he was convicted.

He wondered if Maya Gray would be ready this time.

NOW AVAILABLE!

BROKEN
(A Casey Bolt FBI Suspense Thriller—Book One)

FBI special agent Casey Bolt, with her rare neurological condition, is able to see and feel patterns other can't—and when a winemaker is found dead, victim of a serial killer, Casey must tap her special skill to follow the trail and hunt down a diabolical killer before he strikes again.

"Molly Black has written a taut thriller that will keep you on the edge of your seat… I absolutely loved this book and can't wait to read the next book in the series!"
—Reader review for Girl One: Murder

BROKEN is book #1 of a long anticipated new series by critically-acclaimed and #1 bestselling mystery and suspense author Molly Black, whose books have received over 2,000 five-star reviews and ratings.

Casey, grappling with synesthesia, has the rare ability to perceive senses in multiple ways, enabling her to view crime scenes, and track down clues, in ways others cannot. Her talent has made her indispensable to the FBI, but while her renown in the FBI grows, Casey remains tormented by the case that haunts her the most: her mother's brutal, unsolved murder from fifteen years ago.

As Casey strives to uncover the secrets of the past, she must rely on every instinct and insight to make it out of the field alive. But can her own senses lead her astray?

A page-turning and harrowing crime thriller featuring a brilliant and tortured FBI agent, the CASEY BOLT series is a riveting mystery, packed with non-stop action, suspense, twists and turns, revelations, and driven by a breakneck pace that will keep you flipping pages late into the night. Fans of Rachel Caine, Teresa Driscoll and Robert Dugoni are sure to fall in love.

Future books in the series are also available.

"I binge read this book. It hooked me in and didn't stop till the last few pages… I look forward to reading more!"
—Reader review for Found You

"I loved this book! Fast-paced plot, great characters and interesting insights into investigating cold cases. I can't wait to read the next book!"
—Reader review for Girl One: Murder

"Very good book… You will feel like you are right there looking for the kidnapper! I know I will be reading more in this series!"
—Reader review for Girl One: Murder

"This is a very well written book and holds your interest from page 1… Definitely looking forward to reading the next one in the series, and hopefully others as well!"
—Reader review for Girl One: Murder

"Wow, I cannot wait for the next in this series. Starts with a bang and just keeps going."
—Reader review for Girl One: Murder

"Well written book with a great plot, one that will keep you up at night. A page turner!"
—Reader review for Girl One: Murder

"A great suspense that keeps you reading… can't wait for the next in this series!"
—Reader review for Found You

“Sooo soo good! There are a few unforeseen twists… I binge read this like I binge watch Netflix. It just sucks you in.”
—Reader review for Found You

Molly Black

Bestselling author Molly Black is author of the MAYA GRAY FBI suspense thriller series, comprising ten books (and counting); of the RYLIE WOLF FBI suspense thriller series, comprising six books; of the TAYLOR SAGE FBI suspense thriller series, comprising eight books; of the KATIE WINTER FBI suspense thriller series, comprising eleven books (and counting); of the RUBY HUNTER FBI suspense thriller series, comprising five books (and counting); of the CAITLIN DARE FBI suspense thriller series, comprising six books (and counting); of the REESE LINK mystery series, comprising six books (and counting); of the CLAIRE KING FBI suspense thriller series, comprising seven books (and counting); of the PIPER WOODS mystery series, comprising five books (and counting); of the GRACE FORD mystery series, comprising seven books (and counting); and of the CASEY BOLT mystery series, comprising five books (and counting).

An avid reader and lifelong fan of the mystery and thriller genres, Molly loves to hear from you, so please feel free to visit www.mollyblackauthor.com to learn more and stay in touch.

BOOKS BY MOLLY BLACK

CASEY BOLT MYSTERY SERIES
BROKEN (Book #1)
FLAWED (Book #2)
BLEMISHED (Book #3)
DAMAGED (Book #4)
TWISTED (Book #5)

GRACE FORD MYSTERY SERIES
NEARLY MINE (Book #1)
NEARLY SAFE (Book #2)
NEARLY FREE (Book #3)
NEARLY GONE (Book #4)
NEARLY HIS (Book #5)

CLAIRE KING MYSTERY SERIES
ONCE HE SEES (Book #1)
ONCE HE LONGS (Book #2)
ONCE HE TAKES (Book #3)
ONCE HE FEELS (Book #4)
ONCE HE KNOWS (Book #5)

MAYA GRAY MYSTERY SERIES
GIRL ONE: MURDER (Book #1)
GIRL TWO: TAKEN (Book #2)
GIRL THREE: TRAPPED (Book #3)
GIRL FOUR: LURED (Book #4)
GIRL FIVE: BOUND (Book #5)
GIRL SIX: FORSAKEN (Book #6)
GIRL SEVEN: CRAVED (Book #7)
GIRL EIGHT: HUNTED (Book #8)
GIRL NINE: GONE (Book #9)

RYLIE WOLF FBI SUSPENSE THRILLER

FOUND YOU (Book #1)
CAUGHT YOU (Book #2)
SEE YOU (Book #3)
WANT YOU (Book #4)
TAKE YOU (Book #5)
DARE YOU (Book #6)

TAYLOR SAGE FBI SUSPENSE THRILLER
DON'T LOOK (Book #1)
DON'T BREATHE (Book #2)
DON'T RUN (Book #3)
DON'T FLINCH (Book #4)
DON'T REMEMBER (Book #5)
DON'T TELL (Book #6)

KATIE WINTER FBI SUSPENSE THRILLER
SAVE ME (Book #1)
REACH ME (Book #2)
HIDE ME (Book #3)
BELIEVE ME (Book #4)
HELP ME (Book #5)
FORGET ME (Book #6)
HOLD ME (Book #7)
PROTECT ME (Book #8)
REMEMBER ME (Book #9)
CATCH ME (Book #10)
WATCH ME (Book #11)

RUBY HUNTER FBI SUSPENSE THRILLER
IF I RUN (Book #1)
IF I TELL (Book #2)
IF I LIVE (Book #3)
IF I FORGET (Book #4)
IF I RETURN (Book #5)

CAITLIN DARE FBI SUSPENSE THRILLER
COME GET ME (Book #1)
COME FIND ME (Book #2)
COME TAKE ME (Book #3)

COME CATCH ME (Book #4)
COME SAVE ME (Book #5)

REESE LINK MYSTERY
BEYOND REASON (Book #1)
BEYOND REACH (Book #2)
BEYOND REPAIR (Book #3)
BEYOND DOUBT (Book #4)
BEYOND NORMAL (Book #5)

Printed in Dunstable, United Kingdom

68569883R00087